"Believe me, y̶ ̶ ̶ ̶ ̶ be happy̶ ̶ ̶

Confusion called out from Kevin's piercing brown eyes. "Just spill it, Leah."

As the old adage went, a picture was worth a thousand words, which was why Leah chose to remove the photograph from the clear plastic folder. A photograph that resided among others of friends and family and all those precious in her life, including one of her and Kevin taken during their final vacation in Mexico that for some reason she hadn't had the desire to remove. But this particular photo was the most precious of all.

She dropped the wallet back into her bag and offered the picture to Kevin without explanation. Clarification would come soon enough.

He studied the photo for a time before his gaze snapped to hers. "Who is this?" Her gift. Her miracle. Her entire world.

"She's your daughter, Kevin."

Dear Reader,

After I learned I was expecting my first child, I couldn't imagine how I would handle all the sleepless nights, the countless diaper changes, the absolute fear of failure. Believe me, I had more than a few "what was I thinking?" moments during that pregnancy. But after my daughter's birth, it didn't take long before I couldn't imagine my life without her.

As remarkable as becoming a parent can be, it does tend to alter your schedule, to say the least. You can't always sleep when you feel like it, you don't always have ample alone time. You can't routinely party until dawn or travel cross-country on a whim. After all, an innocent child is counting on you to provide the most basic of needs—food, clothing, shelter and, most important, love. In other words, it is true what they say—having a baby does change everything. And that is what inspired me to write a story about a confirmed bad-boy bachelor, who has made more than his share of mistakes, and his unanticipated journey into fatherhood that leads to his redemption.

I hope you enjoy *His Best Mistake*, where Kevin O'Brien discovers that living for the moment isn't nearly as rewarding as living for the ones you love.

Happy reading!

Kristi Gold

His Best Mistake
Kristi Gold

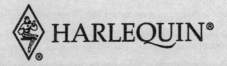

HARLEQUIN®

TORONTO • NEW YORK • LONDON
AMSTERDAM • PARIS • SYDNEY • HAMBURG
STOCKHOLM • ATHENS • TOKYO • MILAN • MADRID
PRAGUE • WARSAW • BUDAPEST • AUCKLAND

Recycling programs
for this product may
not exist in your area.

ISBN-13: 978-0-373-71624-1

HIS BEST MISTAKE

ABOUT THE AUTHOR

Kristi Gold has always believed that love has remarkable healing powers and feels very fortunate to be able to weave stories of love and commitment. As a bestselling author, National Readers' Choice winner and Romance Writers of America RITA® Award finalist, Kristi has learned that although accolades are wonderful, the most cherished rewards come from personal stories shared by readers and networking with other authors, both published and aspiring. You may contact Kristi through her Web site, www.kristigold.com, Facebook or through snail mail at P.O. Box 24197, Waco, Texas 76702 (please include an SASE for response).

Books by Kristi Gold

In loving memory of my wonderful mother,
Jean.

PROLOGUE

"IT'S APLASTIC ANEMIA…it can be fatal…"

As a senior staff writer for a prominent sports magazine, Kevin O'Brien possessed an extensive vocabulary. But the words *aplastic anemia* meant nothing to him. *Fatal* did.

Not five minutes ago, he'd been in his Houston loft packing for a trip after arranging a rare interview with a well-known pro-football player. Now his physician brother was pretty much telling him he could be biting the big one, reaching the finish line and every other clichéd description of death that came to mind.

No way could this be happening now. He had a great career that had been years in the making. He'd been involved in an eight-month relationship with a woman who had come to mean more to him than he'd ever thought possible. He was only thirty-five, and he still had too much left to do to die. But in light of the grave look on Devin's face, he might not have any choice in the matter.

Needing to sit, and fast, Kevin raked a newspaper

from his favorite lounger and dropped down on the chair. "Are you sure about this?"

"I'm positive." After taking a seat on the sofa, Devin leaned forward and said, "You have a dangerously low level of red and white blood cells and platelets. That means you fall into the moderately severe range for the disease."

Kevin thought about how he'd lived life on the edge, driven to achieve prominence in his field, and how sometimes he would exchange sleep to get ahead. He'd also made more than his share of mistakes along the way. "What in the hell caused this?"

"It's idiopathic, which means no known cause. It only happens to about three in every one million people in this country annually."

Lucky me. "So do I just sit around and wait for it to kill me, or is there something you can do to treat this?"

"I'm an E.R. doctor, Kevin, and a relative, so I can't treat you. I only agreed to order the lab work as a favor when you started having the nosebleeds and fatigue. But I know a good hematologist who'll manage your care."

Kevin's anger began to build. Anger directed at his brother who was obviously bent on deserting him, which wasn't exactly logical. But he didn't have a firm grip on logic right now.

He pushed out of the chair and began to pace. "Can't you tell me anything about what I'm facing, Dev, or did Mom and Dad waste all that money on your training?"

His brother held up his hands, palms forward. "Calm down, Kevin."

If he had more energy, he'd put his fist through the wall. "You try remaining calm when someone just handed you a death sentence."

"It doesn't have to be a death sentence. You can have a bone-marrow transplant."

After inhaling a few deep breaths, Kevin reclaimed his spot in the lounger. "What does that entail?"

"You'll have to undergo a process to destroy all your bone marrow before the transplant. That involves roughly two weeks of chemotherapy. Post transplant, you're looking at six months to a year of recovery time. You'll have to limit your contact with the general public until your immune system is back to normal."

Aside from being tired as a dog, Kevin didn't feel all that sick. Therefore, he had no intention of letting this disease interfere with his work. "No way can I consider the transplant for at least three months. Preseason football starts in a couple of weeks and I have at least ten interviews scheduled. I have to make a living."

"Not if you're dead."

His brother's proclamation packed the punch of a right hook. "There's no medicine I can take to stop this?"

Devin sighed. "You could have transfusions for a few months, but that's only supportive care, not a cure. Eventually you'll have to have the transplant in order to survive."

At least that was something positive. But he still had questions. "Does this transplant come with a guaranteed cure?"

"Nothing is one-hundred-percent foolproof, Kevin. The transplant preparation itself poses risks. But if you want a shot at a full recovery, it's your only alternative. Fortunately, you have an identical twin who's a perfect genetic match as a possible donor."

Not an option. Not when he'd barely spoken to his brother over the past few years. "I'm not going to ask Kieran to do that, and even if I did, he wouldn't agree. Give me another choice."

"We could test the other siblings to see if they're a match and I'd be willing to be tested, too. Or you can search for a match through outside donor registries. But with either of those options, you're increasing your chances for rejection."

"I can't expect any of you to turn your own lives upside down for me, so I'll just take my chances and go with the donor registry."

Devin looked as frustrated as Kevin felt. "You're shutting out the family like you always do, Kevin. Don't be so damn stubborn."

"I'm being practical." Practicality had always served him well when it came to masking his emotions. And right now, his emotions were running the gambit from fury to fear. But fear was counterproductive and he vowed not to give in to it. "I don't have time to deal with this now. I have to catch a plane in less than two hours and I have an interview to conduct in about four." Anything to get his mind off the news.

"Cancel the trip and get someone to cover for you, Kevin. Until you see the hematologist and decide on a treatment plan, your immune system can't handle even the slightest infection. Airplanes are breeding grounds for those infections."

Great. Not only had he been presented with the prospect of losing his life, he could very well lose his job. "I've worked too damn hard to establish myself with the magazine to blow it all to hell now."

Devin nailed him with a glare. "A certain amount of denial is expected in this situation, but you'd better start facing reality—and soon. You're sick and you have no chance to get better unless you get the medical attention you need."

His mind wanted to reject that reality, but his gut told him he'd better heed his brother's advice. "I'll cancel the trip."

"Good," Devin said as he stood. "I'll call the hematologist and have him work you in tomorrow. In the meantime, you should talk to Mom and Dad because you're going to need all the support you can get, especially during the chemo phase. It's tough."

If he told his parents now, his mother would immediately warp into overprotective mode, exactly what she'd been doing since the day he'd been born the sickly twin. He preferred to avoid that scenario for as long as possible. "I'll wait to tell Mom and Dad until I know exactly what's going to happen next."

"Fine, but don't wait too long, Kevin. And there's one more thing you need to know. You have a fifty-fifty chance of being sterile because of the chemo. If you're serious about your girlfriend, you need to discuss this with her. But since she's a doctor, she'll be able to help you sort through all the information."

Right now Kevin was on information overload, yet one thing had become all too clear. He couldn't burden Leah with his problems, not when she was so close to finishing her fellowship. Not when he might not be able to give her the one thing she'd always said she wanted—a lot of kids. More important, if the treatment failed to cure him, he didn't want her to watch him die. "Leah and I broke up." A lie, but he planned to make it the truth, and soon.

"I'm sorry it didn't work out," Devin said. "And I'm sorry I never got to meet her. I hear she's a nice lady."

She was more than nice. She was the best thing that had ever happened to him.

His brother walked to the exit but paused before opening the door. "I'll notify you later today when I have an appointment time. Try to get some rest and call me if you need me, even if it's only to talk."

"Thanks, Dev. I appreciate it."

"You bet. And one more thing. It's okay to be afraid."

When Kevin couldn't come up with a response, his brother walked out the door, leaving him alone to plan what he needed to do next, and that involved making several phone calls.

He thought about canceling his flight first and contacting the magazine after that. But one call took precedence over the others, and it happened to be the one he dreaded the most.

Better to get it over with now, before he had time to reconsider. He walked into his office and picked up the phone, clutching the receiver in his hands for a few seconds before he hit the speed dial that would connect him with the hospital where Leah spent most of her time.

After he waited several minutes for her to answer the page, she greeted him with her usual, "Dr. Cordero."

Just the sound of her voice filled him with overwhelming regret. "Hey, Leah. It's Kevin."

"I didn't expect to hear from you so soon. From what you told me this morning, I thought you'd be on your way to Dallas about now. Is your flight delayed?"

"No. I just wanted to talk to you."

"I'm glad you called. It gives me the chance to say goodbye to you twice in one day."

He was about to say goodbye permanently, and that was tearing him up inside. "I have something I need to tell you."

"Is everything okay, Kevin? You sound strange."

He was anything but okay. He might never be okay again. "Look, Leah, I've been thinking, and the truth is, my life is crazy right now, and so is yours. I've decided it's better if we take a break for a while."

A span of silence passed before she said, "A break? Or do you mean break up?"

He brought out all the old excuses that he kept on hand like a favorite pair of worn jeans. "It's getting too serious between us. I'm not ready to settle down, and I doubt you are either."

"I see. So this *is* the infamous break-up speech.

Might have been nice if you'd taken the less cowardly route and told me in person."

If he'd done that, she would've sensed he was lying, and he might have buckled under her scrutiny. "I'm busy, Leah."

"But not too busy to whisk me away on a four-day resort vacation a week ago?" She released a bitter laugh. "What was that, Kevin? A few last-minute screws just for grins? And all those things you said about how much you cared about me. I should've known better than to believe you."

At the time he'd meant every word he said. God, he still did. "I do care about you, Leah."

"And I hate you for doing this to me, Kevin."

He could hear the tears in her voice and despised the fact that he'd put them there. "I'm sorry." A totally inadequate statement, but the only thing he knew to say.

"I'm sorry, too. Sorry we ever met and that you turned out to be such a bastard. Heaven help the next woman who becomes involved with you."

When she hung up the phone, Kevin experienced an overwhelming sense of loss the likes of which he'd never known. Although he still believed he had no choice but to let Leah go, he couldn't help but wonder if he'd just made the greatest mistake of his life.

What life he had left.

CHAPTER ONE

O'Brien's Sports Scene
June Edition

OVER THE past several months, I've learned one important lesson—facing death will definitely change your life...

He immediately highlighted the text and punched the delete button with a vengeance. He had no business personalizing a syndicated column targeting a readership focused on fantasy teams, play-off berths and trade deadlines. But the fact that he'd even considered revealing his life-and-death battle to the general public indicated exactly how much his life had changed. How much *he* had changed.

During his battle with the disease that had nearly killed him, Kevin had become much more introspective, more settled. Hell, he'd even bought a house in a Houston suburb. A year ago, he never would've envisioned exchanging cross-country jet-setting for a home office. If he hadn't gotten sick, he wouldn't have spent so much time contemplating his mistakes, either, and he'd made plenty. One particular mistake continued to haunt him daily, but he couldn't dwell on that decision now. Not if he wanted to make his Monday-morning deadline.

When the doorbell chimed, Kevin leaned back in his chair and released a rough sigh. Most likely his mother had dropped by unannounced to question why he hadn't attended the traditional O'Brien Sunday lunch, when in reality she'd come to make sure he hadn't suffered a relapse. As much as he appreciated her concern, he'd become increasingly annoyed by her obsession over his well-being. Then again, Lucine O'Brien had that obsession down to a fine art where he was concerned.

The bell sounded again and for a moment Kevin contemplated ignoring the summons. Not a good idea. His car was parked in the drive, which could cause his mom to panic and place an unnecessary call to the paramedics. Leaning to his right, he pulled back the curtain to the window facing the front lawn. But instead of finding his mother's minivan parked at the curb, he caught sight of another car. A very familiar car.

No way could it be her. First of all, she didn't know where he lived. Secondly, she hated him, which is what she'd said verbatim the last time he'd spoken to her by phone all those months ago. Then again, he didn't know another solitary soul who owned a cherry-red Volkswagen convertible.

Curiosity sent Kevin to the front entry to seek verification that his past had in fact landed on his doorstep.

Verification that came when he peered through the side-light window and laid eyes on the woman standing at the edge of the walkway, motionless, as if her feet were frozen to the cement.

He'd recognize that body from a football field away, even though it was encased in a loose, flowing, sleeveless aqua dress instead of her standard scrubs. He couldn't mistake those exotic, almond-shaped hazel eyes that almost matched the tone of her skin. He'd witnessed those eyes grow heavy and hazy when he'd made love to her—and darker when he'd riled her temper. He also couldn't forget that silky, brown, chin-length hair streaked with blond, either. He recalled in great detail how it had felt against his bare skin.

From the moment he'd met her, Dr. Leah Cordero had become one of his major weaknesses. Not only was she beautiful and smart, she had been the best lover he'd ever known. Sexy as hell. Wild and uninhibited. Incredible. The kind of woman who brought a man to immediate attention. Every part of him.

And he'd better make damn sure he was decent before he faced her again, which is why he waited a few moments before opening the door. He also needed time to assess why she might have sought him out. Maybe she'd decided to give him another piece of her mind, this time in person. Maybe she'd somehow learned he'd been sick, the lie he'd lived with—and almost died with—for twelve long months. And just maybe, if luck prevailed, she wanted a second chance. And believing that would make him the ultimate fool.

LEAH HAD only one reason to confront Kevin O'Brien, even though she'd been tempted to hold off the revelation until another day. Yet she'd recently decided that taking the high road seemed the prudent thing to do. Unfortunately, it didn't look as though she'd get the chance to speak her mind today because either he wasn't at home or he was avoiding her. That meant she would have to return later, if she didn't lose her nerve.

Leah started back to her car but paused in the middle of the walkway to turn and take one last look at the massive abode Kevin had purchased in her absence. An amazing house, to say the least. And the fact he'd settled in a family-friendly neighborhood was also remarkable. That caused her to question whether he lived with someone, namely, a woman.

Frankly, what Kevin O'Brien did or didn't do wasn't any of her concern. He could live with ten women, for all she cared. He didn't matter to her anymore…at least that's what she thought until he walked out the front door and came toward her.

As hard as she tried to ignore the impact Kevin still had on her, Leah couldn't. Couldn't ignore his steady, self-assured gait, his aura of strength—it had captured her attention the night they'd met in a premier Houston nightclub on one of the very rare occasions when she'd been out on the town. She surely couldn't ignore the longer length of his hair or the shading of whiskers on his normally clean-shaven face, although those unexpected aspects didn't detract from his incredible looks. But she had to remember her mission. Remember that what had once existed between them had ended in the span of a three-minute phone conversation almost a year ago.

Kevin paused a few feet before her and hooked his thumbs into the pockets of his jeans. "Hey," he said in a voice that sounded almost remorseful.

Leah mustered all the fortitude she possessed, using recollections of their last verbal exchange to bolster her courage. "Hello, Kevin."

He sized her up with one lengthy, slow visual excursion. "You look great."

So did he. Nothing better than a sexy man dressed in white T-shirt and faded jeans. But she didn't plan to pay him any compliments, even if she did intend to be coolly polite. "Do you have a few minutes to talk?"

"I'm all yours."

At one time, Leah had honestly believed that. But not now. Not ever.

When she noticed a few people milling around the front lawn next door, she decided the last thing she needed was an audience when she lowered the boom. "Can we go somewhere more private?"

"We can go inside," he said. "I'll give you the grand tour."

"I wouldn't want to bother anyone else who might be inside."

Kevin frowned. "I'm the only one here."

"You don't have a roommate?"

"Nope. It's just me."

At least that answered her question. Still, she didn't

dare spend a moment alone in a house with Kevin O'Brien. Particularly in a house with a bed. Or a sofa or a floor, for that matter. "I'd prefer the front porch."

"It's a lot cooler in the house, Leah." He studied her through narrowed eyes. "Or are you afraid I'm going to make a move on you if we're alone together?"

Yes, and equally afraid she might forget that he'd trampled her emotions and make an inadvisable move on him. "That wouldn't be a first, Kevin."

"You know me well enough to know that I won't do anything you don't want me to do, Leah."

Aside from breaking her heart. "I still think remaining outside would be better."

His expression showed a hint of impatience. "Could we at least go into the backyard and sit in a chair under some shade?"

That sounded like a solid plan to Leah. Kevin might need a chair once she was done. "Okay."

He gestured toward the drive to his left. "Right this way."

"Just a minute." Leah returned to the car, opened the door and grabbed a bag from the backseat. A bag that contained two items representing her reasons for the spontaneous visit.

After slipping the strap over her shoulder, she walked with Kevin down the lengthy drive, keeping a reasonable berth between them. Even a brush of arms would bring about old memories she didn't care to relive, although at times she had relived them in her mind. Each wonderful, exciting and heartbreaking moment. She'd foolishly been bowled over by his easy charm, intrigued by his complex personality. Completely drawn in by his expertise as a lover. She'd learned quite a bit about him in their eight months together. Clearly she hadn't learned the most important detail before she'd fallen totally in love with him—he wasn't in the market for a permanent commitment.

Once they rounded the corner of the house, Kevin opened a black iron gate that provided the entry through a white brick wall surrounding the backyard. When he motioned her forward, Leah stepped into what she would deem a perfect oasis, right down to the rock waterfall feeding into a crystal-blue diving pool and a state-of-the-art outdoor kitchen adjacent to a small cabana.

"Wow." That was the only thing Leah could manage around her surprise.

"Pretty great, huh?"

She turned and caught Kevin's smile. Big mistake. That smile had been the death of her determination to resist him on more than one occasion. After a brief mental pep talk, Leah said, "It's very nice. Great for entertaining."

"Yeah, but I haven't had a chance to do much entertaining yet. I've only been here a month."

As if she really believed a month wasn't enough time for him to entertain various bikini-clad beauties. "Corri told me you'd only recently moved in." The only solid information his sister-in-law had provided when Leah had worked up the nerve to contact her.

His smile faded into a frown. "Is that how you found me?"

"Yes. I called her after I stopped by your loft and discovered you'd moved."

"Didn't she give you my new phone number?"

"She did, but I decided we needed to speak in person." She'd actually considered delivering the news by phone, affording him the same non-courtesy that he'd afforded her when he'd ended their relationship. Instead, she'd opted to be an adult and engage in a face-to-face meeting, although at the moment she questioned her wisdom.

But she was here now, so she might as well get down to brass tacks. On that thought, she asked, "Can we sit down now?"

"Sure." Kevin guided her to a table situated beneath a copse of pines and oaks and pulled out a brown-striped chair.

Leah took the designated seat while Kevin chose the chair across from her, thankful for the table that put much-needed space between them. She set her bag on the ground at her feet and tightly clasped her hands on the glass surface. "These trees help with the heat." At least from a meteorological standpoint. Noticing all of Kevin's finer details didn't help Leah's internal heat in the least. It seemed he'd lost some weight, but he'd undeniably gained some muscle. He'd always been in great shape, but his biceps looked larger. His chest looked broader. His abs looked tighter beneath the T-shirt. And if she knew what was best, she'd keep her eyes off his attributes.

"The Houston heat in June's always brutal, especially at four in the afternoon," he said, drawing her attention back to his face.

"I had a busy morning, otherwise, I would have been here much earlier." She'd spent the better part of the day engaged in an internal debate, until she'd forced herself to stop procrastinating.

After another brief bout of silence, Kevin asked, "How's your fellowship going?"

Though she was avoiding the news she'd come to deliver, Leah saw no reason not to be civil. "It's going well. The hospital rotations can be tough, but I work part of the time in a clinic."

"Which means more normal hours," he said.

Odd that he remembered all the details they'd discussed during their time together. Then again, he had been very attentive, both in and out of bed. "I'm really looking forward to finishing in August so I can finally start utilizing what I've learned." She would have been finished now had she not taken a necessary break in her hometown before returning to Houston two months ago.

Kevin brushed a leaf from the table with a sweep of his hand. "Have you decided where you're going to practice?"

In some ways, that decision had been made for her. "I'm going home to Mississippi. Since my fellowship has focused on healthcare for the indigent, I plan to work part-time in a free clinic, and possibly open my own practice to pay the bills."

"You won't miss the big-city lifestyle?" His tone

hinted at disappointment, or maybe she was reading too much into it.

"I'd miss my family more." She also needed their support, now more than ever.

"I'm sure you'll do great, wherever you land," he said. "Good luck."

For some reason, she'd wanted him to say he would miss her. That he'd made a huge error in judgment by letting her go. That he wished she would stay in Houston. And that was insanely ridiculous. Even if he did say all those things, she couldn't believe him.

The conversation died for a time until Leah sent a quick glance in his direction to find him rubbing his eyes. "You look tired. Obviously you've been burning the midnight oil." Or burning up the sheets with his latest babe.

"Just been busy with work."

"Traveling a lot?"

"Actually, no. For the most part I'm working from home now. I write a nationally syndicated column and I maintain a sports blog for the magazine."

That surprised her almost as much as the longer length of his hair. "You've always loved interviewing all those sports superstars. What on earth happened?"

His expression showed definite discomfort. "Things change, Leah."

Yes, but she suspected he hadn't. Maybe he wasn't traipsing all over the country searching for his next female conquest, but she had no doubt women were still seeking him out on a regular basis, and he was gladly accommodating them. That didn't matter to her any longer, or it shouldn't.

She'd come here to say something important, and she needed to say it now. Yet when Kevin centered his dark eyes on her, Leah temporarily misplaced her train of thought. And when he leaned over and traced a fingertip along her jaw, she stiffened and muttered, "Don't."

If he so much as touched her again, Leah might momentarily forget how badly he'd wounded her, heart and soul. She refused to do that. Refused to succumb to his charm that he wielded like a net to ensnare unsuspecting females. She'd already been there and she wasn't going back.

"Sorry." His features turned sullen as he once more leaned back in his chair. "Do you mind telling me why you're here?"

"Not to take up where we left off, Kevin." Lying wasn't the norm for Leah. In fact, she always demanded honesty under normal situations. Yet nothing about this situation was normal. She'd do whatever seemed necessary to discourage him, even if that meant fabricating an intimate relationship with another man. "Besides, I'm seeing someone."

Kevin leaned forward and studied her a long moment. "Who is he?"

Leah was taken aback by the question, as well as the jealousy in his tone. A typical male I-don't-want-you-but-I-don't-want-anyone-else-to-have-you reaction. As it was with her job, she had to think quickly. "He's someone I've known for a long time. We met up again when I was visiting my parents in Mississippi." Not exactly a lie, but not the whole truth, either. She had seen her childhood friend, J. W. Camp, a few times when she'd been home. But J.W. was more like a brother to her, a detail she chose to omit. "He owns his own business. He's a good man. Solid. Steady. Honest."

"And you don't believe I'm any of those things?"

At one time, she had. "It doesn't matter what I think, Kevin. It's over between us."

"Is your relationship with this guy serious?" He sounded almost dejected.

Leah started to issue a denial, but reconsidered. "Look, Kevin, I'm not here to talk about my personal life with you. But we still have something very important to discuss."

"Then talk. I'm listening." His tone held a touch of anger, very unlike the Kevin she'd known before. He was usually all about gentle persuasion, deadly charm, but now he seemed much more serious. Or maybe he simply wished she would get out of his life for good.

That's precisely what she'd planned to do—to stay out of his life—as soon as she presented her actual rationale for being there. With that in mind, she opened the bag, withdrew her wallet and held it firmly in her grasp. "First of all, I've agonized for weeks over what I'm about to tell you," she began. "I've spent a lot of sleepless nights trying to figure out exactly *how* to tell you. But a few days ago, it occurred to me that putting it off any longer wouldn't make it any easier. You're still going to be mad."

He sent her a cynic's smile. "That would be a switch, you making me mad instead of the other way around."

Leah could only pinpoint one time when he'd made her mad—furious in fact—and that had been the day he'd called it off between them without fair warning. "Believe me, you're not going to be happy about this."

Confusion called out from Kevin's piercing brown eyes. "Just spill it, Leah."

As the old adage went, a picture was worth a thousand words, which was why Leah chose to remove the photograph from the clear plastic folder. A photograph that resided among others of friends and family and all those precious in her life, including one of her and Kevin taken during their final vacation in Mexico that for some reason she hadn't had the desire to remove. But this particular photo was the most precious of all.

She dropped the wallet back into her bag and offered the picture to Kevin without explanation. Clarification would come soon enough.

He studied the photo for a time before his gaze snapped to hers. "Who is this?"

Her gift. Her miracle. Her entire world. "She's your daughter, Kevin."

CHAPTER TWO

KEVIN LOOKED as stunned as Leah had been when she'd confirmed the pregnancy all those months ago. She waited patiently for his verbal reaction, and when she didn't receive one, she said, "Her name is Carly." Named for Carl, the little boy her parents had fostered when Leah had been in her teens. A special little boy no one had wanted because of his myriad medical problems. But Leah had loved him dearly, had helped care for him until the day he went into the hospital and never came out. He'd been the reason she'd chosen pediatrics as her specialty, but Kevin knew that. Not that he would remember.

Kevin stared at the photo before centering his gaze back on her. "How old is she?"

"Three months."

"And you're just now telling me?"

She'd considered not telling him at all, but she'd changed her mind after her mother reminded her of all the children who'd come to them with no medical histories, no knowledge of their own parents. "I called you a week or so after I confirmed the pregnancy. Some woman answered and I hung up. I planned to call you the month Carly was due, but before I could do that, I went into labor four weeks early. It all happened very fast."

He looked alarmed. "Is she okay?"

"She's fine. Perfect. A little underweight, but she's catching up."

He ran a hand through his hair. "I don't know how this happened. We were always careful."

"Not always, Kevin. Remember that wild time we had on our trip to Cabo last summer?" The trip where Kevin hadn't been himself. She'd learned the reason for his attitude a week later when he'd dumped her. "I had one too many margaritas the last night we were there. You had too much testosterone."

"But I—"

"Not quickly enough. Besides, we both know that coitus interruptus is not a fail-proof form of birth control." Yet that night she hadn't been thinking clearly, and it had had little to do with alcohol because she hadn't been intoxicated. The overriding passion between them had been the only thing that mattered. A passion that had often clouded her common sense.

When he still seemed doubtful, Leah added, "All you have to do is look at her, Kevin. She's the mirror image of you." So much so, she ached every time she looked at her baby girl. *Their* baby girl.

"Where is she now?" he asked as he continued to focus on the photo.

"With my roommate, Macy." All the more reason why Leah needed to leave as soon as possible, before the baby woke from her nap and Macy—a confirmed kid phobic—had to deal with Carly.

Kevin stared at the picture a few more moments, and when Leah couldn't stand the silence any longer, she said, "Say something."

He leveled his gaze on hers. "I don't know what to say, Leah. This is one helluva shock."

She understood that all too well. She also acknowledged that he might have a difficult time coping with the news. He might decide not to cope with it. For that reason, she retrieved an envelope from the bag and offered it to him. "Here."

After a brief hesitation, he took it from her. "What is this?"

"It's a document that will terminate your parental rights if you sign it. You're under no obligation to be involved in her life, emotionally or financially."

A flash of dismay crossed his expression. "After everything you've told me about the abandoned kids your parents fostered, you're willing to raise her by yourself?"

If she had a choice, Leah would prefer raising her child in a two-parent home. But that wasn't an option, at least not with Kevin. "We're doing fine." For the most part. "I also have a good support system at home."

"You mean your new boyfriend."

Leah opted not to comment on that supposition. "My parents insist I move back in with them when I return to Mississippi. You don't need to worry about whether or not Carly's going to be cared for if you decide to sign the papers."

Without offering any response, Kevin lowered his head, the envelope and photo still in his grasp. He appeared so visibly shaken, Leah fought the urge to hold him.

Instead, she gathered her things and stood. "I realize this is a lot for you to think about, so I'm going to give you that time to think. If you'd prefer to walk away from this situation, I'll understand. All you have to do is sign the documents, have them notarized and mail them back to me in the envelope I've provided. I've already addressed it. In the meantime, I have the same cell number if you need to reach me."

It took all of Leah's strength to leave without any answers from Kevin. She wasn't certain what to hope for—that he sign the papers to sever his parental rights, ending their relationship, once and for all, or that he decide to be a father to Carly, gaining a permanent place in his child's life—her life—for years to come. Either way, she would have to deal with the consequences of her actions. Her mistakes.

But Leah didn't view her baby as a mistake. Falling in love with Carly's father had been a grave mistake. Thing was, a part of her still loved him, and probably always would.

SHORTLY AFTER DAWN the following morning, Kevin traveled to Bodies by O'Brien, the health club owned by his twin brother, Kieran. His reasons behind the visit were twofold—a workout to clear his mind and counsel from someone he could trust.

Even though he'd barely slept the night before, adrenaline sent Kevin through the double doors at a quick clip and straight to Kieran's office where he found his brother seated behind his desk.

"Do you have a few minutes?" Kevin asked as he stood in the open doorway, clutching his gym bag in a death grip.

Kieran looked up from a stack of papers and tossed the pen aside. "Come in. You're saving me from approving invoices, and you know how much I hate the business end of the business."

Spoken like a die-hard personal trainer, Kevin decided. But saving Kieran from accounting was a far cry from what Kieran had saved Kevin from—certain death—by providing his bone marrow. The ultimate gift, as far as Kevin was concerned. Since that time, they'd put aside their differences and had become as close as they'd been when they were kids, one of the few positives resulting from his illness.

Kevin crossed the room and dropped down in the chair in front of the desk. He decided to ease into the conversation while preparing to get into the crux of the matter at hand. "How's it going with the wedding plans?"

Kieran smiled. "At least we finally have a place to have it, which is good considering the ceremony's in less than a month."

"Where did you decide to do it?" Kevin asked.

"Logan's father-in-law offered his garden. It's going to be damn hot, but Erica wants an outdoor wedding.

And it shouldn't be too bad at sunset. Are you still willing to stand up for me under those conditions?"

"You bet." Kevin would gladly brave the elements to fulfill his duty as Kieran's best man, although he'd never really been "the best man." Not even close.

Kieran inclined his head and sized him up. "If you don't get a haircut before the wedding, people won't be able to tell us apart. I don't want my bride kissing the wrong man."

Kevin ran a hand through his hair and laughed. "I'll keep that in mind. In the meantime, I'm going to let it grow out. I kind of want to hang on to it a little longer since I lost so much during the chemo." The same chemo that could have altered his chances of having a child, which reminded him of why he'd come to see his brother.

In preparation for the boom-lowering, Kevin drew in a deep breath and let it out slowly. "Leah came by the house yesterday."

Kieran leaned back and rubbed a hand over his jaw. "I'll be damned. What did she want?"

Kevin reached into his gym bag, pulled out the items Leah had given him yesterday and offered the photo to Kieran. "She brought me this."

Kieran took the picture and stared at it for a long moment before he turned his attention back to Kevin. "Is this what I think it is?"

"If you're thinking that's my daughter, you'd be right." *My daughter.* Never in a thousand years would he have believed he'd be saying that. Nor did he expect to feel what he'd felt after learning the news.

"She looks exactly like our baby pictures." Kieran shook his head. "Man, this is a shock."

"Yeah. What a way to start a week." What a way to change your life in a matter of minutes.

Kieran laid the photo on the desk and slid it toward Kevin. "I can't believe Leah waited this long to tell you."

"Considering what I did to her, I can't really blame her. And as it turns out, she did try to tell me. She hung up when some woman answered, and I'm fairly sure that woman was a home health-care nurse who was giving me transfusions at the time. But I understand why she would assume otherwise."

"She assumed she'd been replaced," Kieran said.

Kevin couldn't fault Leah for that, either. "She was going to try to tell me again right before the baby was born, but she went into premature labor."

Kieran frowned. "The baby's okay?"

Exactly the same thing Kevin had asked the baby's mother. "She's healthy, according to Leah. And since Leah's a pediatrician, she should know."

Kieran grinned. "As far as I'm concerned, Kev, this is damn good news. I say tell Leah the whole story, and maybe you'll get another chance with her."

If only that was a possibility. If only he'd done things differently, told her about his illness instead of using his pat confirmed-bachelor excuse. If only he hadn't done irreparable damage to their relationship by trying to protect her, maybe he wouldn't be in this predicament now. Then again, he wasn't certain he would do anything differently, even knowing what he knew now. The last thing she'd needed during a pregnancy was dealing with his problems. "I don't see any reason to tell her the whole story."

"You can dole out the advice, Kevin, but you can't follow it."

Kevin couldn't remember giving his brother any advice worthy of notice. "What are you talking about?"

"When you were in the hospital, you told me I needed to drop my guard and confide in Erica or risk losing her. I did that, and look how well it turned out. Now you have a chance to do the same thing, and you're not even going to try."

"There's no point in trying. It wouldn't change anything."

"Why do you think that?"

Because a few major issues still prevailed. Issues that prevented Kevin from attempting to win Leah back. "First of all, Leah hates lying and even if my intentions were good, she'd have a hard time buying it. Secondly, she wants a big family, and I might not be able to give her that because of the chemo."

"Why don't you let her decide if that matters?"

On to the most important issue. "It's too late for us, Kieran. She's already involved with someone from her hometown. I'm pretty sure he's the reason why she's decided to set up practice in Mississippi once her fellowship is done. And I'm also sure that's why she gave me this." He held up the envelope. "If I sign on the dotted line, I'll terminate my parental rights."

"You're not seriously considering that, are you?" Kieran looked and sounded incredulous.

Kevin had seriously considered it all through the night. Yet every time he thought about walking away from his daughter—a child he had yet to see, the only child he might ever have, he hurt like hell. He hurt just as deeply when he thought about walking away from Leah. Again. "On the one hand, I keep telling myself no way would I let another man raise my child. On the other, maybe that would be the unselfish thing to do. Maybe I'm not cut out to be a father."

"Just don't make any rash decisions until you take one more important step," Kieran said.

Kevin suspected his brother was about to ask him to do something he wasn't prepared to do. Not until he knew which road he was going to take. "If you're going to say I need to tell Mom and Dad about the baby, I'm not ready to do that."

"That's not what I was going to say."

Kevin's impatience was nearing the breaking point. "Then just say it, Kieran, so I can go work out."

"Forget the workout. Go see your baby girl, Kev."

"THERE'S SOMEONE here to see you, Leah."

At the sound of her roommate's announcement, Leah looked up from Carly, who'd drifted to sleep at her breast. "I didn't hear the doorbell."

Macy moved into the room and secured a band around her wavy blond hair. "That's because he didn't ring the bell. I was on my way out when I found him standing on the doorstep, looking like a stray dog."

Leah suspected she knew the identity of that stray dog. "Did you manage to get his name?"

"I didn't bother, but I can tell you what he looks like. Dark hair, dark eyes, good-looking in a slick kind of way. Come to think of it, he looks just like her." She pointed toward the still-sleeping infant in Leah's arms.

Oh, great. "Leave it to Kevin to show up unannounced," Leah muttered, though she had no cause to criticize him. Yesterday she'd done the same thing.

Macy's eyes widened. "Kevin, as in the baby-daddy Kevin?"

"That's the one."

"I thought you weren't going to tell him."

"I changed my mind." Or lost her mind, as the case might be.

When Leah moved the baby to her shoulder and stood, Carly released a little whine of protest. "Hold her for a minute. She needs to be burped."

Macy looked as if Leah had asked her to perform an appendectomy on the dining-room table. "I don't know nothin' 'bout burpin' babies."

Leah grabbed a towel from the side of the rocker, draped it over Macy's shoulder and handed Carly over. "Just pat her back a couple of times."

When the baby released a moderate belch, to say Macy looked frazzled would be a grave understatement. "What if she hurls on my scrubs?"

"That's what the towel's for, but she's not going to

hurl." Leah, on the other hand, fought a twinge of nausea over the thought of facing Kevin.

After buttoning her blouse, she took Carly back into her arms, popped a soft kiss on her cheek and laid her in the bassinet positioned next to her bed. "Tell him I'll be right out as soon as I'm presentable."

Macy scowled. "Who cares what you look like? He's the sperm donor, not your prom date."

Ignoring her friend, Leah moved in front of the bureau's mirror and ran a brush through her hair. "Be that as it may, he's still Carly's father."

"He's a jerk, Leah. He doesn't deserve to be a father."

Leah stared at Macy from the mirror's reflection. "You've never even met him."

"But I know what he did to you, and that makes him an A-one jackass in my book."

Leah turned and leaned back against the bureau. "Just tell him I'll be with him in a minute, okay?"

Macy shrugged. "Fine. Mind if I kick him in the jewels on my way out? If I do it hard enough, that could prevent him from procreating again."

Leah pointed the brush at the door. "I would prefer you deliver my message without any violence and then go to work."

"You're absolutely no fun," Macy said as she did an about-face and marched out of the room.

Going back to the mirror, Leah took a long look at her appearance and grimaced. Her face showed the signs of fatigue, right down to the bloodshot eyes. Balancing a baby's needs and a busy schedule had begun to take its toll. She applied a little lip gloss then scolded herself for believing she had to make herself up to see Kevin. Macy was right; this wasn't a date. At least not in the traditional sense. A date with destiny could be in the offing, depending on Kevin's reasons for showing up unannounced.

She walked back to the bassinet to find Carly still snoozing, her fists balled up at her chest, a smile playing at the corners of her mouth. Evidently her daughter was having a sweet baby dream, completely unaware that the man responsible for her birth was waiting in the next room.

Leah wondered if Kevin would ask to see his child. If so, maybe she should change Carly into something more appropriate than the yellow, hand-me-down sleeper. Another silly idea. Carly was an infant, for goodness sake, and she wasn't required to impress her father. If Kevin couldn't see past his daughter's apparel to the blessing beneath, then Macy was right—he didn't deserve to be in Carly's life. As if he really wanted to be involved with his baby, something she genuinely doubted.

After drawing in a deep breath, Leah walked into the tiny living room to discover Kevin seated on the floral chintz sofa, looking somewhat weary. He also looked incredibly handsome in an expensive navy silk suit with a white tailored shirt, sans tie. She hated the flutter of awareness, the remembrance of a time when she would have greeted him with a kiss. Hated that he could still move her so easily into those memories, those feelings that were best left unfelt.

"A phone call might have been nice," she said on the heels of her exasperation. "But then you were always full of surprises, Kevin." Some very nice surprises, and some not so nice.

He came to his feet, his gaze fixed on hers. "I had an appointment downtown this morning. Since I was so close, I decided to stop by."

That explained his business apparel, even if it didn't provide all the answers Leah required. "How did you find us?"

"Your address was on the envelope you gave me, remember?"

Actually, she hadn't remembered. "Did you have a business meeting?"

"I met with my accountant." He pulled an envelope from the inside of his jacket pocket. "This is the outline of the trust fund I'm setting up for Carly. The actual documents haven't been drawn up yet because I want you to look over this first and make any changes. You'll have complete access to the funds and if you need more, you only have to tell me."

After a brief hesitation, she took the envelope from him. "As I've said before, I don't expect you to be financially responsible for Carly if—"

"I know what you said, but she is my responsibility, and I want to provide for her."

Leah wondered if a monetary obligation was the only tie he planned to have with his baby. Still, she'd gladly accept anything that would give her child a better life, at least until she had all the student loans paid off and her private practice up and running. "I'll take a look at it and get back with you. Anything else?"

"I'd like to see her."

At least that answered one of Leah's questions, and prompted some concerns. But now that she'd involved Kevin in the situation, she had no good reason to deny him, particularly when he seemed so sincere. "She was sleeping when I left her a few minutes ago, but I guess you could take a peek."

Leah led Kevin into her bedroom that also served as the nursery. When she moved to the bassinet, she discovered her daughter wasn't sleeping at all. Instead, Carly was intently focused on the multicolored mobile dangling above her.

Leah sent a quick glance over her shoulder to see Kevin standing near the door, as if uncertain what he should do next. "She's awake, so you can come closer."

He took his place beside Leah and stared down on Carly, who favored him with a smile, as if she somehow sensed he was a special guest.

"She's started smiling a lot in the past month," Leah said.

Kevin didn't respond, but the awe in his eyes spoke volumes. "She's beautiful."

Leah couldn't agree more. "She's a good baby, as long as she's fed and dry. But she does have an occasional bout of mild colic and a little bit of a temper that comes out when she doesn't get what she wants right away."

He remained quiet for a time before asking, "May I hold her?"

Leah certainly hadn't prepared for the question, even though that would be a logical request from a first-time father. Regardless, she gestured toward the rocker next to the crib. "Have a seat and I'll hand her to you."

After Kevin complied, Leah lifted the baby from the bed and laid her in the crook of his arm. Carly smiled at him again and Kevin smiled back. "Hey, kiddo. I'm your dad," he said, his voice soft, almost reverent.

Leah couldn't count the times she'd envisioned this scene, under very different circumstances. She'd often engaged in the happy-family fantasy of three. A pipe dream that would never come to pass, even now. But she couldn't refute how natural he looked holding his daughter. Couldn't discard the surge of emotions, the threat of tears as Kevin closed his eyes and pressed his lips against Carly's forehead as he held her close to his heart.

This beautiful man, who had never mentioned wanting children, looked as if he, too, was battling his own emotions over seeing his child. But Leah had to remember this was only one special moment. Possibly a goodbye moment.

A brief time later, Kevin slowly stood and laid the baby back in the bassinet. When he faced Leah again, he pulled another envelope from his pocket. "I stayed up most of the night thinking about these papers." He opened the flap and withdrew the document. "And here's what I really think about them."

After setting the envelope on the rocker, he turned, systematically shredded the paper and tossed the remains into the nearby trash bin. "She's my daughter, Leah, and I want to be a part of her life. I *need* her in my life."

When Leah was able to speak around her shock, she asked, "You're absolutely sure about this?"

"Yes, and I want to prove it."

Leah hugged her arms tightly to her midriff. "How do you propose to do that?"

"By taking care of her while you're working."

And Leah had just thought she couldn't be more astounded. "That's not necessary. I have her enrolled in a good day care."

"And I have a flexible schedule—I can devote my time to her."

This proposition was almost more than she could digest. "Do you understand what that entails, Kevin? All the feedings and changing and bouts of endless crying?"

"I understand that completely, and I'll handle it. And now that I'm here, there's something else I want to address." He looked around the area, focusing on the double bed crammed into the corner. "Does Carly have her own room?"

"It's only a two-bedroom apartment, and I have a roommate, which is why Carly's in here with me."

He sent her a sly grin. "Oh, yeah. Your roommate. The one who looked like she wanted to castrate me before she left."

At least Macy hadn't delivered the groin kick. "She's nice when you get to know her."

He gave her a *Yeah, right,* look before surveying the room again. "I don't know a lot about babies, but isn't Carly going to outgrow that bed soon? And it seems to me you don't have room for a bigger one."

That ruffled her maternal feathers. "This apartment is all I can afford right now, Kevin, and I promise you that she'll have a full-size crib when the time comes, even if I have to sleep on the floor."

He looked altogether cynical. "That's a great idea, Leah, sleeping on the floor. I'm sure that's going to provide you with a lot of rest before you have to make life-or-death medical decisions."

Leah recognized he had a point, and she had another suggestion. "Then I'll sleep on the sofa."

He cracked another crooked smile. "The one with the flat cushions? That's going to be great for your back, which if I remember correctly, bothers you if the bed's too firm."

When exasperation began to surface, Leah bordered on demanding his departure. "Again, I'll make do for the next two months. Carly won't suffer in any way, shape or form."

"I'm thinking there's a better solution that will prevent any suffering or sacrifice for either of you."

Leah was almost afraid to ask. "What would that be?"

"A new place to live. A better place."

"I've told you I can't afford—"

"At my expense."

She mulled that over for a moment, greatly tempted

by the offer. Kevin was a financial wizard with a portfolio that rivaled any corporate CEO's. Many times he'd given her fiscal advice and ways to plan for her future after her fellowship. He had the funds to finance a bigger apartment. A place where Carly could have her own nursery, allowing Leah to sleep in her own bed. "You're really serious about paying my rent for a bigger apartment?"

"Not an apartment. A house."

Maybe even in a neighborhood with a park where Leah could take the baby on her days off. The deal was getting sweeter by the moment. "A house would be great, but all the homes near the hospital are incredibly expensive."

"I was thinking more along the lines of a newer subdivision about fifteen minutes out. A great house in a great neighborhood. Four bedrooms, four baths, almost four thousand square feet. Gourmet kitchen and a big backyard with a pool."

Leah laughed. "That's a little bit of overkill for two people, don't you think?"

"Three people."

Leah swallowed hard. "I'm not sure what you're getting at, Kevin." In reality, she knew exactly what he was getting at.

And he confirmed her suspicions when he smiled and said, "I'm talking about my house, Leah. I want you and Carly to move in with me."

CHAPTER THREE

"ARE YOU serious?"

Kevin wasn't at all surprised by Leah's reaction, even if he was surprised by his own spontaneous offer. But come to think of it, the whole idea made perfect sense. "I'm dead serious."

She sent him a champion scowl. "You've lost your mind, Kevin."

Possibly for thinking she'd actually agree to it. But he wasn't willing to give up…yet. "It's a good arrangement, Leah. You can go to work in the mornings without having to drop Carly off anywhere. I can take care of her during the day and you can take over when you come home at night if you're not too tired. Hell, I can even have dinner waiting for you."

Her skepticism showed in her expression. "You don't cook."

"Not true. I made you dinner one night at my apartment."

She smiled. "You heated up a dinner that your sister-in-law was kind enough to prepare for us."

Kevin returned her smile, mostly from remembrance

of one of many great evenings they'd shared. "You didn't complain. In fact, I don't remember you issuing any complaints the entire night." Or in the morning, when he'd made love to her again for the second time. Or maybe it had been a third time...

Leah cleared her throat, jerking Kevin back into the present. "Lack of cooking skills aside, exactly what do you know about taking care of a baby?" she asked.

Not much. "I have several nieces and nephews that I've taken care of a time or two." Under direct supervision from their parents during family get-togethers, a detail he'd rather not reveal at the moment in light of Leah's cynical look.

When Carly whimpered, Leah scooped the baby up in her arms and laid her on the bed. "Hand me a diaper and the wipes," she said as she began to undo a maze of snaps down the legs of Carly's footed pajamas.

Kevin looked around a few moments before Leah added, "The box is in the corner and the wipes are on the dresser."

He retrieved a disposable diaper and a plastic container clearly indicating baby wipes. After handing the items to Leah, he sat on the edge of the mattress next to his daughter.

"Do you want to do this?" Leah asked, looking expectant.

If he even made an attempt, then he'd prove just how little he did know. "Since we've only recently been introduced, I'll watch while you change her."

"You haven't done it, have you?"

She was too damn intuitive for her own good. For his own good. "No."

"That's what I thought," she muttered as she untaped the diaper, slipped it from beneath Carly, rolled it up and tossed it into the nearby pail.

Kevin tried to concentrate on the rediapering task, but he was distracted by the baby noises Carly began to make. "Did you hear that?" He sounded as if his daughter had just recited the preamble to the Constitution.

"She started the cooing phase a week ago," she said as she refastened all the snaps with the skill of a baby-changing artist.

When Carly smiled at him again, Kevin said, "She sure is a happy girl."

Leah picked up the baby and held her against her shoulder. "She's not going to be happy for long since it's past time for her nap."

That was his cue to leave. He stood and said, "Fine. I'll go so she can take her nap. I'll call you later to discuss the move."

"I didn't say I was going to move in with you, Kevin."

At least she hadn't said she wouldn't, which meant he still had a shot at pleading his case. "Just think about how convenient it would be if we lived together."

She laid the baby back in the bassinet then turned and sent him a wry smile. "It's not the convenience that worries me."

He knew exactly what was worrying her—the possible fallout from their proximity. "Listen, I have two master suites, one on each end of the house, with two bedrooms in between. One of those rooms would be Carly's. And you'd have your own private bath, with a whirlpool tub." Hell, now he sounded like a real-estate salesman.

"I'm sure it's nice, Kevin, but I'm not interested."

"Aren't you even the least bit tempted?" He brought out the big guns—a wink.

Leah rolled her eyes, indicating he'd lost his ability to entice her. "Temptation got us into this situation in the first place."

He couldn't argue that point. He did intend to argue his case for cohabitation. "You wouldn't have to be around me unless it involved Carly. In fact, you'll be gone most of the day, which leaves only a few hours at night when you'd have to tolerate my presence."

"True, but frankly, I'm not sure I trust you even for five minutes."

He battled a bite of anger, even knowing he'd done nothing to earn her trust to this point. "Look, Leah, you're going to be moving in August. That gives me less than two months to get to know my baby before you take her out of state. I can't do that when she's in a day care all day."

"You can still see her before I leave and after I move to Mississippi, provided that's what you want."

"You mean every other weekend? Maybe a holiday or two? That's not a hell of a lot of time for us to build a relationship."

She sighed. "We'll work it out later. Right now your daughter needs to sleep."

Your daughter. That alone fueled Kevin's determination. He'd give Leah some space and in the meantime, he'd prepare for the best-case scenario—having Leah and Carly in his home—even though he wouldn't be stunned if she refused him. "Okay," he said as he backed toward the bedroom door. "I'll be in touch in a few days. Call me if you change your mind before then."

"I'm not going to change my mind, Kevin."

THE MINUTE her roommate breezed through the front door, Leah could no longer maintain her silence. "You're not going to believe what Kevin did."

Macy laid a hand across her forehead with all the polish of a practiced drama queen. "With a baby on the premises? Has he no shame?"

Leah blew out a frustrated breath. "He asked me to move in with him."

Macy dropped down on the sofa and leaned her head back against the cushion. "Please tell me you didn't agree, Leah."

"Of course not." Although admittedly, she'd thought of nothing else but Kevin's proposition for most of the day.

"Good. For a minute there, I thought you'd lost your mind," Macy said as she toed out of her clogs.

Leah took the chair opposite Macy and propped her heels on the coffee table. "He says it would only be temporary. Just until I move back to Mississippi in August."

Macy frowned. "If you're not going to do it, then why are you telling me this?"

Leah didn't understand why revealing the details to

Macy seemed so important, but it did. "I only want you to realize that it's not what you think. Kevin wants to get to know Carly, and I can't very well keep him from her now that I've involved him in her life."

"*Her* life," Macy added. "Those are the key words. That doesn't mean you have to shack up with him. He can have her for a few hours during the weekend."

That sounded logical, yet Leah acknowledged why that might not seem adequate to Kevin. "He also offered to watch her during the day while I'm at work."

Macy smirked. "You must not think too highly of your kid, leaving her in the hands of a monument to bad influence."

Leah regretted telling her roommate all the unflattering details of Kevin's past. "He's not an ogre, Macy."

"No, he's a player who probably has a revolving door in his bachelor boudoir."

Leah fell silent a few moments before she continued. "He owns a house with four bedrooms, four baths and a pool."

Macy perked up like a puppy awaiting a treat. "A pool? Wading or in-ground?"

"In-ground. With a waterfall and a hot tub."

"Well, heck, you stay here with the baby and I'll move in with him."

Leah was astounded at the sudden spear of jealousy hurling through her over that thought. "He's not your type, Macy."

"Yeah, I know. He's much too pretty for me. I prefer a less refined guy. Someone who's good with his hands."

"Kevin's definitely good with his hands." Among other things.

Macy leaned forward and nailed Leah with a serious stare. "I honestly believe you're considering his proposition."

"Absolutely not." Realizing the sheer defensiveness in her voice, Leah tempered her tone. "You're right. Pool or no pool, it wouldn't work."

Macy tugged the band from her hair, sending a blond crop of curls cascading down her shoulders. "Maybe you're worried it *would* work. Maybe you're afraid you'll get reeled in again. But hey, nothing wrong with convenience sex, as long as you don't let all that emotional garbage enter into it. And as long as you double up on the condoms."

"I'm not in the mood for any kind of sex." Not exactly a lie. She hadn't even thought about sex for months…much. "Besides, I've told him I'm seeing someone."

Macy's mouth hung open a few moments before she snapped it shut. "When do you have time to see anyone?"

"I don't and I'm not. I only want him to believe that I'm off the market."

"What are you going to tell him if he asks for details about this mystery man?" Macy asked.

"I've already covered that. I'll pretend my new lover is J.W., my friend from Mississippi."

Macy snorted. "You mean that mechanic who called here one night and told me he had a really big toolbox then asked if I wanted to check it out?"

Good old J.W. "Yes, but don't worry about him. He's all hat and no cattle."

"Huh?"

"He's all talk and no action."

"I'll take your word for it." Macy slapped her hands against her thighs and stood. "I have to hit the shower now because I *am* in the mood for a little lovin'. I have a date with some prime beef tonight and he's picking me up in less than an hour."

Leah experienced some unwarranted and unwanted envy. "I'll vacuum so he doesn't injure his knuckles when they drag the floor."

Macy rolled her eyes. "You do that, Leah. And just one more question. Did you make it clear to Kevin that you're not interested in playing the happy-family game with him?"

"I tried, but knowing Kevin, he's not going to let it go easily." In fact, Leah wouldn't put anything past him.

"I NEED to borrow one of your kids."

After the declaration spewed out of Kevin's mouth, he'd give a month's pay for a camera to capture the confused look on his brother-in-law's face.

"What in the hell are you talking about, Kevin?"

"If you'll let me in the house, Whit, I'll tell you." He didn't relish the thought of explaining the situation to his sister, Mallory, but desperation had sent him across Houston during rush-hour traffic for some much-needed assistance.

After a moment's hesitation, Whit held open the door and muttered, "Come in."

Kevin entered the living room to find Mallory seated on the edge of the sofa wearing a pink silk robe. A bottle of champagne and two glasses were set out on a hideous, hairy rug covering the hardwood floor. A cozy scene indicating an intimate celebration. His timing royally sucked.

"Is something wrong with your cell phone, Kevin?" his sister asked, her tone less than amicable.

He shoved his hands in his pockets and tried to look contrite. "Sorry. I just assumed that since it's six o'clock on a Monday, I wouldn't interrupt anything but dinner."

"It's almost seven." Whit dropped down next to Mallory and rested a hand on her thigh. "If you'd shown up five minutes later, I wouldn't have answered the door."

Kevin eyed the spread on the floor. "Is it your anniversary?"

"No." Mallory tightened the robe's sash and moved closer to her husband. "Whit found out today he's going to design a multimillion-dollar home for a prominent corporate CEO. We're celebrating."

Kevin offered his hand to his brother-in-law for a shake. "Congratulations."

Whit smiled with pride. "Thanks. I beat out a dozen other architects, so I'm pretty happy about it. I'll begin working on the design in a few weeks."

"Sounds like a good deal," Kevin said. "Who is this tycoon, anyway?"

Mallory sighed. "Let's cut the chitchat, you two. And Kevin, what are you doing here?"

"He wants to borrow one of the girls," Whit said before Kevin could respond.

Mallory scowled. "What for?"

Now came the nitty-gritty. The explanation that might take a while. With that in mind, Kevin selected the club chair across from the sofa and prepared to confess. "I'll try to be brief."

"Good idea," Whit said. "We have to get back to the celebration and you're not invited to watch."

Kevin launched into the details of his reunion with Leah, learning about Carly and his most recent proposition. He concluded by saying, "She hasn't agreed to move in with me yet, but even if she doesn't, I still want to learn how to take care of the baby. That's why I'm here."

As soon as the astonishment left Mallory's expression, she leaned forward and folded her hands in her lap. "Does this mean the two of you could possibly get back together?"

Obviously he'd been born into a family of frustrated matchmakers. "No, it doesn't. She's not interested."

"Even after you told her about your illness?" she asked.

"I haven't told her, and I don't intend to."

Whit shook his head. "You're making a huge mistake, bud."

Maybe so, but Kevin didn't intend to complicate matters any more than they already were. "I have my reasons for keeping the information to myself."

"I can't imagine what they might be," Mallory said. "If she knew why you broke it off with her, then I'm sure she would be willing to give you another chance."

Kevin was too mentally stressed to get into his motives now, especially since he'd already hashed them out with Kieran that morning. "Take my word for it, telling her wouldn't matter. But I still want to do right by my daughter, and that's where the twins come in."

Mallory folded her arms across her middle. "First of all, as much as I'd like to loan you a child, Lucy and Maddie are with Mom and Dad for the night. Secondly, they're potty-trained, off the bottle, on solid foods and out of a crib. In fact, they're going on three, not three months. I kind of doubt they'll be of any help, unless you need all the particulars about the latest and greatest cartoon characters."

Damn. He hadn't considered that his nieces were beyond the infant stage. "That just goes to show how much I know about kids."

Mallory came to her feet and waved a hand at him. "Come with me. I have an idea."

Whit groaned as Kevin followed his sister out of the den and into the hall. They traveled several feet before reaching a bedroom decorated in shades of yellow and green, twin beds—not cribs—set out on opposing walls. Mallory crossed the room, picked up a doll and two miniature diapers from a shelf, turned and offered them to him. "You can practice with Sally Sweetness, who happens to be anatomically correct. If you'd like, I can give you one of her play bottles. Fill it up with water, stick it in her mouth, and in a matter of minutes, she'll wet her diaper and you can change it."

Not at all what he'd had in mind. "A doll isn't the same as the real thing, Mallory."

"It's a start, Kevin. Or you could wait another few weeks for Logan and Jenna's baby to arrive."

He didn't have weeks to wait for the birth of another niece or nephew. Not if he wanted to prove to Leah that he could care for Carly now. He took the doll from Mallory and stuffed the diapers in the pocket of his slacks. "I'll make do with this."

"I just remembered something else that might help, so wait here," Mallory said as she left the room. She returned a few moments later, this time with a book that she held out to him. "You'll find everything you need to know about babies in here."

He took the book and flipped through the pages, complete with illustrations. "It's all covered in here?"

"Yes, but if you have any questions, call me. You can also call Mom. After all, she's raised six kids."

Not something he cared to do. "I don't want to tell Mom and Dad yet. Not until I know for certain if Leah's going to go along with my plan."

Mallory inclined her head and studied him for a moment. "You don't want Mom hovering, which is why you came to me instead."

His sister knew him too well. "You could say that. I want to do this on my own, or at least for the most part. But I have to admit, it's pretty daunting."

She patted his arm. "You're a smart guy, Kevin. And

don't let anyone fool you into thinking that men don't have instincts when it comes to their children. All you have to do is listen to those instincts, and love your child."

The odd thing was, Kevin already loved Carly, even though he'd only held her one time. "I'll remember that."

Mallory studied him a few moments before saying, "Believe it or not, I think you're going to make a good father, Kev."

Then his sister did something totally unexpected—drew him into a hug. The moment seemed awkward at first, at least to Kevin. He'd built a lot of walls during his adulthood, even when it came to his family. Especially when it came to family. But he welcomed the renewed closeness with his siblings, now more than ever.

After Mallory released him, Kevin smiled self-consciously. "Wish me luck with convincing Leah that moving in with me would be the best thing for all three of us."

Mallory grinned. "You don't need any luck, Kevin. You only need to turn on that charm you've always used to your benefit."

Kevin didn't feel all that charming lately. "That was the old me, Mallory. I'm not sure that person exists anymore."

"Oh, I think he does. Only he's a better version of that person."

Kevin sincerely hoped he had become a better person. More important, he hoped that Leah would eventually recognize that. "Thanks, Mallory."

"Not a problem. Again, if you decide you need my help with anything else, let me know. Only next time, call before you drop by."

Kevin could think of one thing he really needed—a miracle. Nothing short of that would convince Leah to move in with him.

"PLEASE go to sleep, sweetie." Leah recognized how foolish she sounded, pleading with a thee-month-old infant. But she was growing more desperate by the minute, as well as losing what little coherency she had left.

No matter what she'd attempted in order to lull her baby to sleep—from a drive around town, feeding her several times and rocking her for what seemed like hours on end—nothing had worked.

Using all her medical knowledge, she'd examined Carly from head to toe, taken her temperature and determined that her daughter wasn't in any physical distress. She basically didn't care to sleep, despite her mother's exhaustion. She continued to teeter between wide-eyed bouts of glee and fits of nonstop fussiness. Worse still, the behavior had gone on for three nights in a row. Of course, the day-care workers had reported that Carly had been the perfect little angel, napping twice during the day for at least two hours at a time. Unfortunately, Leah hadn't had that luxury. She did have an impending schedule crammed full of appointments with children who needed her skill and her attentiveness. At this rate, she wouldn't be able to form a complete sentence, much less perform an accurate well-baby check.

When Carly started to cry again, Leah rose from the rocker and strolled around the room, feeling as if she'd lost control of her life. She'd worked so hard to be a competent pediatrician, but she obviously lacked in parenting skills.

If only she could close her eyes for a few minutes, or at the very least take a shower to get a head start on the morning. And morning would be arriving in less than two hours.

On that thought, Leah left the room with Carly in her arms and headed down the hall to seek out her roommate. Macy could at least watch over Carly long enough for Leah to get a quick bath and maybe a nap. Provided Macy was open to the plan.

Once she reached Macy's room, Leah quietly opened the door so she wouldn't startle her. Carly picked that moment to let out an irritable howl, as if she sensed her mother was about to foist her off on a woman who didn't possess one solitary maternal bone in her body.

A sliver of light fell across the bed, illuminating Macy's closed eyes. "I really could use some help," Leah whispered.

Macy groaned, lifted her head and muttered, "What time is it?"

"Almost four. Carly's been up most of the night and I haven't had any sleep. Could you watch her for an hour or so while I take a nap?"

Macy rolled onto her back and sighed. "I'm scrubbing in on an open heart in less than five hours."

Leah wasn't in the mood for a schedule competition, but she'd do whatever she had to do to earn Macy's assistance. "And I have to see the first of thirty or so kids in less than four hours."

"Sorry. My mitral valve trumps your rug rats. If I'm not on my game, Brannigan will find some way to punish me for at least a month. Isn't that right, Dr. Lattimer?"

"Damn straight," came from beside Macy in a decidedly low, masculine tone.

Only then did Leah realize that Macy had a bed buddy. A playboy anesthesiologist, to be exact. Somehow Macy had sneaked him into the apartment. Probably when Carly was screaming at the top of her lungs.

Leah murmured, "Sorry to bother you," as she closed the door on the scene. And Carly smiled up at her, as if she found the situation very amusing.

Leah wasn't amused. She was weary and tired and a little jealous of Macy. Not that she would trade her child for a casual fling. Not that she wanted to have a life without Carly, no matter how difficult raising a baby alone could be.

Yet as she returned to the tiny room and began to rock her daughter again, she fought back tears. The urge to cry strengthened when she considered her former relationship with Kevin and how she had hoped for a future with him.

Leah might have been wrong about that, but she wasn't wrong about one thing—Kevin did care for their child. He'd proven that the moment he'd held Carly. He'd affirmed that when he'd set up a trust fund and then offered his home to them. And remarkably, he hadn't pressured her into making a decision about the move since he'd made that offer six days ago.

The longer Leah weighed Kevin's proposition, the more she believed that it could be best for both her and the baby. She would actually have some help on nights like these, when she felt as if she were failing as a parent. When she felt so alone.

With Kevin, she might find some stability for the time being, or at least until she moved to Mississippi. And when that time came, she would be the one to leave, instead of the other way around. That should give her some satisfaction, yet Leah only felt sad, and that's when the tears began to fall in earnest, soft and quiet like the bundle in her arms.

Leah listened to the sound of Carly's steady breathing and realized she'd finally fallen asleep. But she didn't dare try to put the baby down for fear she'd awaken again. Instead, she leaned her head back against the rocker and closed her eyes. Yet, before fatigue completely overtook her, she came to a decision. For the sake of her mental health, her career and, most important, her daughter, she was going to move in with Kevin. And now that she'd made up her mind, she only had one more decision to make—exactly how and when to tell him.

CHAPTER FOUR

"Okay, I'll do it."

Kevin's sleep-induced stupor prompted the only logical response to the woman's abrupt declaration. "You'll do what?"

"Move in with you."

When the mental fog cleared, Kevin scooted up against the headboard and swiped a hand over his face. "Leah?"

"Yes. How many women have you invited to move in with you?"

Oh, hell. "None. I'm just surprised to hear from you after midnight." Or at all, for that matter.

"You used to rarely go to bed before two."

True, but that was before he'd gotten sick. Now he made it a point to be in bed by midnight, as long as he wasn't facing a tight deadline. "It's been a crazy week."

"Tell me about it."

She sounded exhausted and maybe that had to do with the decision she'd made. And to think that after a week of no contact and no indication that she'd changed her mind, he'd almost given up. A week when he'd decided to back off in hopes that she'd come around. Apparently that had worked. "Are you sure you still want to go through with it?" Damn. Now he sounded like *he* wasn't sure.

"Yes, unless you've reconsidered."

"Not at all." Not in the least.

"Okay," she said. "But before we go any further, we need to set some ground rules."

Kevin didn't find that at all unexpected. Leah had always been about order and rules, and he'd broken more than a few in their relationship, including his promise always to be honest with her. "Go ahead. I'm listening."

"I don't have much time, so I'll just cover a few of the most important ones. I expect your daughter to wake up any moment now, something she's been doing every two hours lately."

No wonder she sounded tired. "Guess she inherited your insomnia."

"I don't consider myself an insomniac."

"I remember a couple of times when you couldn't sleep. One time in particular, not long after we'd started dating. You called me at 3:00 a.m. and asked if you could come over." And they'd been all over each other the minute she'd walked through his door. They hadn't even made it to the bedroom. Hell, they hadn't even made it to the couch. Nothing like a hot stop, drop and roll on the carpet... "Do you still have those zebra-striped silk pajamas?" The ones she'd worn to his house that night, covered by a coat. Great pajamas. Thin-strapped top, low-riding bottoms, man-slaying effect.

"That's the first rule, Kevin. No trips down memory lane."

Too late. He'd already traveled down the recollection road. "I'm just curious." His innocent tone didn't sound all that convincing, and he doubted Leah was convinced, either.

"I threw those pajamas away over a year ago," she said.

Probably around the same time he threw away their relationship. "What about the other rules?"

She cleared her throat as though she was preparing for a serious speech. "No touching. No late-night conjugal visits when the baby's asleep."

Double damn. "You make it sound like you're condemning me to prison."

"No. I'm just making myself perfectly clear when it comes to my expectations. And I'm going to keep Carly in day care until I know for certain you can handle her."

He tightened his grip on the receiver. "Good idea. I might forget she's there and toss her out with the recyclables."

"As I've said before, I have some trust issues with you, and trust is earned, Kevin."

He probably merited her scorn, and that only fueled his determination to prove himself competent enough to care for their baby. "What if I pick her up early in the afternoon, say an hour or two before you get home?"

A brief span of silence passed before she said, "I suppose that might work. *After* we've been there for a few days and I see how well you handle her. Babies are not easy."

At least he was making some minor headway. "Okay, but I'll be glad to take over Carly's care at night, under your supervision, of course. That way you can make sure I'm doing everything correctly."

"I might agree to that, as long as you listen to what I have to say."

"Deal." He would weigh every word she said if it meant having his daughter nearby. Having Leah nearby wasn't unappealing, either, even if she was bent on keeping him at arm's length. "When do you want to move in?" He sounded as eager as a baseball player waiting to hear the all-star selections.

"I'm off next weekend, so I'll pack up then if that suits your schedule."

"That should work," he said, although he only had a few days to prepare. That didn't matter. He'd find a way to make it happen, even if it meant asking for help. "I guess I'll see you on moving day."

MOVING DAY rolled around much quicker than Leah had expected. Between work and caring for Carly, she'd somehow managed to pack her belongings in boxes that were now stacked near the front door. And with Macy's help, she'd loaded most of the baby gear into the car.

At the moment, she was perched on the edge of a chair, waiting for Kevin to arrive to retrieve the rest of her belongings. Carly slept in the safety seat at her feet, totally unaware that she was about to move into a house with the father she barely knew. A month ago, Leah would never have imagined such a thing. A year ago, that had been her secret wish—living with Kevin—only under more favorable circumstances. She would just have to learn to accept a modified, temporary version of that wish.

Dressed in blue-green scrubs covered by a lab coat, Macy breezed out of her bedroom and plopped down on the sofa across from Leah. "Do you have everything?" she asked as she draped her hospital ID around her neck.

"I think so." Leah leaned over, retrieved an envelope she tucked into the diaper bag's outer pocket and offered it to Macy. "Here's some money for my part of the bills. Let me know if I owe more."

Macy waved a hand in dismissal. "Keep it."

"I insist. I'm already leaving you in the lurch by moving out before you've found another roommate."

"I'm not looking for another roommate, and I don't need your money."

That was news to Leah. "I thought you invited me to move in because you did need the money."

"Not hardly. Money has never been a problem for me. Not when my daddy owns half the real estate in New Hampshire."

Oddly, Leah had never pegged Macy as being a "rich" girl, in spite of her socialite looks, but then she really knew very little about her personal history. "What about your mother?"

"She's in charge of spending Daddy's money. Why do you think she named me after a department store?"

Leah chuckled before returning to her next question. "Okay, so if you didn't need the extra income, then why did you ask me to be your roommate?"

"Because I knew Jan was finished with her residency, which meant you wouldn't have a roommate when you came back to Houston after you had the baby. I just figured you needed somewhere to go and I didn't want to step on your pride by letting you stay here free." Macy grinned. "But please don't publicize it. I wouldn't want my fellow docs to think I'm anything less than a heartless drill sergeant."

"My lips are sealed."

Macy leaned forward and nailed Leah with a serious stare. "I'm sorry about the other night."

The sleepless night that had prompted the decision Leah hoped she didn't live to regret. "Don't worry about it, Macy. You're an adult and you're free to do whatever you please with whomever you please."

"I'm not talking about Dr. Feel Good. I'm referring to objecting to watching Carly. To be honest, kids scare me."

She'd always known Macy lacked in motherly skills, but kids scared her? "I didn't think anything scared you, Macy, much less a ten-pound infant."

"Look, I grew up as an only child, and not always a pleasant one at that. Even my imaginary playmates stopped coming around after awhile."

Leah laughed. "I'm glad you've decided to concentrate on surgery, not pediatrics."

"Not in a million years. I'm much better with people when they're completely grown and under sedation."

"You're too hard on yourself, Macy. I've seen a softer side of you." Leah had witnessed that just a few minutes ago.

Macy looked chagrined. "Again, let's not spread that rumor at the hospital. But remember, if your arrangement doesn't work out, you can always come back here. And if Kevin gets out of hand, let me know and I'll bring my scalpel over and turn him into a eunuch with a couple of speedy snips. He'll never know what hit him."

"That won't be necessary. I can handle Kevin."

When the doorbell rang, Leah remained rooted in place, unable to move even an inch. Before she could ask her roommate to let Kevin in, Macy had already made her way to the door and stood peering through the peephole.

"Oh, no. There's two of them."

Leah finally came to her feet. "Two of what?"

Macy sent a quick glance over her shoulder. "Two of Kevin. Unless I've developed binocular diplopia in the last five minutes."

Curiosity sent Leah to the window to take a peek. She confirmed Macy's observation when she saw Kevin and his clone standing on the stoop. No wonder her friend thought she was suffering double vision.

After closing the shade, she said, "That's Kieran, Kevin's identical twin." The twin Leah had yet to meet due to the bad blood that had existed between the brothers. Obviously the feud had come to an end at some point in time.

Macy took another look through the peephole.

"Okay, I see the difference now. The other one has arms as big as a petroleum barrel."

"That's because he's a health-club owner and personal trainer."

Macy grinned. "Where do I sign up?"

If someone didn't answer the door soon, Kevin might decide she'd changed her mind. "Why don't you let him in the apartment so you can ask?"

"Good idea." Macy opened the door, stepped aside and merely said, "Enter."

Both men moved into the living room, making the limited space seem very small. The similarities in their features were remarkable—the same brown hair and intense dark eyes—yet Leah could tell them apart, and not because Kieran carried more bulk. She just knew Kevin that well, his mannerisms and his smile, which he sent her when their gazes met. She hated that sliver of awareness, that sense of excitement he could still generate in her. She recognized the threat in that and vowed to quell those feelings.

Kevin gestured toward his brother. "Leah, this is Kieran. Kieran, Leah."

"It's nice to finally meet you, Kieran," Leah said as she offered her hand for a polite shake.

"Same here," he said. "Kevin's told me a lot about you."

Macy stepped forward and regarded Kieran with a look that couldn't be mistaken for anything other than incontrovertible lust. "I'm Macy, surgeon extraordinaire and Leah's soon-to-be ex-roommate."

Kieran hesitated a moment before taking Macy's offered hand. "Nice to meet you both."

"We need to start loading up ASAP," Kevin said. "Kieran has to leave to pick out a wedding cake."

Macy looked completely crestfallen over the information. "Wedding cake?"

Kieran smiled with pride. "Yeah. I'm getting married in August."

Without formality, Macy pointed at the boxes. "In that case, that's her stuff. I have to go to work now." She turned to Leah. "I'll see you at the hospital." Then she pointed at Kevin. "And you be nice to her and the kid."

With that, Macy strolled to the door but before she left, she shaped her fingers into scissors and sent Leah a snip-snip gesture along with a wily grin. Fortunately for Leah, Kevin and Kieran were too busy surveying the boxes to notice.

"Is this all there is?" Kevin asked as he turned to Leah.

"That's it," she said. "Most everything in the apartment belongs to Macy."

When Carly began to fuss, Kevin crossed the room and crouched down in front of the safety seat. "Hey, baby girl."

"She's been napping most of the morning." Due to the fact that she'd had another restless night, much to Leah's chagrin.

Kieran walked over and stood above Kevin. "There's no doubt she's an O'Brien, Kev. She looks just like us."

Kevin glanced up at Leah and smiled again. "Yeah. But I see a lot of her mother in her."

She should probably thank him for that, but she was more interested in getting the move started before Carly began to protest her confinement. "My car's full of her stuff, but I might have room for a few more boxes."

Kevin straightened after kissing Carly's cheek. "I've got enough room in my SUV for everything."

Funny, as long as Leah had known him, he'd always preferred smaller, sleeker vehicles. "Since when do you drive an SUV?"

"Since I realized my two-seater doesn't have room for a car seat."

"Oh." All Leah could think to say at the moment. The reality of Kevin's role in Carly's life—in her life— was starting to sink in. That reality would become more apparent as soon as she stepped into his house.

LEAH HAD EXPECTED his house to be nice. She didn't expect it to be so incredible—from the soaring ceilings to the muted taupe walls to the polished hardwood floors. Yet nothing in the great room looked familiar. Not the overstuffed beige leather sofa and chair. Not the black accent tables and contemporary artwork. Especially not the photos of his family set out on the mantel above the stone fireplace.

It was as if he'd erased all evidence of his former life as a bachelor living in an upscale condominium sparsely decorated with hodgepodge furnishings. This place seemed much more refined. Better equipped for a couple, but not necessarily a toddler. No matter. She would be long gone before Carly reached that stage.

"What do you think?" Kevin asked as Leah stood in the middle of the room, taking in the scene.

She set down the diaper bag on the sofa along with the safety seat containing her daughter, who'd slept blissfully throughout the trip. "I think it's amazing. Did you design it yourself?"

"With my brother-in-law's help. He's an architect so I told him what I wanted and he drew up the plans."

"You mean Whit." Clearly he'd forgotten she'd met him.

"Yeah, Whit." Kevin looked around a moment as if uncertain what to do next. "Do you want me to unload the boxes now or do you want the grand tour?"

Blatant curiosity had been nagging at her since she'd pulled into the gated drive. "The tour sounds good." She decided to first release Carly from the confines of the car seat and lifted her up onto her shoulder, careful not to wake her. "After you."

They crossed the lengthy great room where Kevin paused at the adjacent kitchen. "The microwave gets the most use in here," he said with a smile.

Such a shame, Leah thought as she studied the immaculate stainless-steel refrigerator and black-granite countertops. And such a waste of a double oven, not that she cared to volunteer to put it to good use. "Is that the laundry room?" she asked when she caught sight of a louvered door.

"That's the main one. There's another washer and

dryer in a smaller room near the second master suite. I'll show you that in a minute."

When Kevin gestured her forward, Leah followed him past another living area that reflected some of Kevin's former life. A curio cabinet housed his numerous journalism awards and a lot of sports paraphernalia—signed footballs and such. A row of theater chairs faced a massive flat-screen TV suspended on one wall.

Kevin turned toward her and continued to walk backward. "This is the den where most of the action happens."

When Carly began to stir, Leah patted her back. "Action?"

"Where I watch all the games. I also have a media area adjacent to the master bedroom."

She didn't dare request to explore that area. "Where to now?"

"Your room."

Kevin led her into a small corridor that ended in a lengthy hallway jutting out right and left. He paused and opened what looked to be the first of a series of doors. "This is the guest bath."

Very lucky guests, Leah thought as she viewed the cocoa-colored marble counters and brass fixtures. "Very nice."

Kevin shut the door and continued down the hall to their right. Once he reached the end, he opened another door. "This is your room."

Leah walked inside ahead of Kevin, her mouth agape. The place was adorned in varying hues of blues, including a king-size bed. A bed that looked all too familiar. "Is this your bedroom suite from the condo?"

He rubbed a hand over the back of his neck. "Yeah. I bought a new set for my room, so I decided to put this one in here since I'd barely owned it a year."

"I know when you bought it," she said, an obvious edge in her tone. "I helped you pick it out."

"Yes, you did."

Great. Now she'd have to retire and wake up in a bed that she and Kevin had put to good use many, many times. She remembered some of those moments in great detail— Kevin's expertise, the heat of his mouth, his feather-light touch, the weight of his body. She quelled the urge to shake her head in an effort to dislodge the images.

Kevin cleared his throat, drawing Leah back into the present, a place she should never leave again. He brushed past her and opened another entry. "As promised, your whirlpool bath."

As soon as Leah stepped onto the white tile covering the floor of the huge bathroom, Carly lifted her head and whimpered, as if she too couldn't believe their good fortune. "I wouldn't know what to do with this much space."

Kevin sent her a half smile. "You'll figure it out. Now let's go see my favorite room."

No way, no how. Not after her previous remembrances. "Kevin, I really don't need to see your bedroom."

"I meant Carly's room, Leah."

Her face heated over her erroneous assumption. "Then lead the way."

Again Leah followed behind Kevin while Carly began to wriggle restlessly against her. Perhaps the baby was excited over the prospect of new sleeping quarters, a ridiculous supposition since a three-month-old only looked forward to one thing—eating.

To say the nursery was totally amazing would be a colossal understatement. The room had been meticulously decorated in tones of muted purple, including a butterfly-bedecked comforter covering a round white crib with a matching canopy. Every imaginable stuffed animal lined a small daybed set beneath an arched window draped with frilly lilac curtains.

Leah turned to Kevin and smiled. "This is unbelievable. How did you get all this done in a week?"

"I had some help."

No doubt from some woman, considering the noticeable feminine touch. "Your current girlfriend?" Now why on earth had she asked that? In truth, she didn't want to know.

"I don't have a girlfriend," he said. "And even if I did, I wouldn't trust the decorating to just anyone, so I asked Mallory. She jumped in and took over, although I had the final say on her decisions."

Leah was caught between unwelcome relief that he was unattached, and concern over how his sister had taken the news about the arrangement. In the limited time she'd been around Mallory, she'd grown to respect her greatly. "She did a wonderful job, Kevin. What did she say when you told her about Carly?"

"She was surprised, but she's dying to meet her. I

told her we'd find a night in the near future to have dinner with her and Whit, if that's okay with you."

"Of course." She could handle dinner with people she'd considered friends before her breakup with Kevin. "What about your mother and father? How are they taking the news about the baby and the move?"

Kevin's gaze faltered. "I haven't found the time to tell them."

Most likely he hadn't found the fortitude to tell them. Although Leah had never met his mother and father, she did know they were traditionalists and might not look too kindly on her and Kevin living together. Of course, they weren't living together in *that* way, nor would they be. Not if she kept her wits about her.

When Carly began to fuss, Leah said, "I think someone needs a diaper. Do you mind getting her bag for me?"

"Not necessary." Kevin walked to an armoire in the corner and opened the doors to shelves stocked with everything a baby could ever need, and then some.

He pulled a diaper from the top of one stack, a plastic tub of baby wipes and a pink changing pad that he laid on the daybed. "Give her to me and I'll do it."

Shock prevented Leah from moving for a moment. "Are you sure?"

He patted the bed and smiled. "Yeah. I've been practicing."

"On one of your nieces or nephews?"

He seemed suddenly ill at ease. "Actually, on Sally Sweetness, one of my niece's dolls."

She wouldn't necessarily qualify that as solid experience unless the doll magically squirmed. But Kevin looked so determined, Leah didn't have the heart to refuse him.

She laid Carly on the pad and pulled the little pink and white bloomers from her bottom. The baby glanced at her before turning her complete attention to Kevin, who'd seated himself on the edge of the mattress. "I might not be as fast as your mom, kiddo," he began as he removed the diaper. "So you're gonna have to be patient with your old dad."

Leah kept a reasonable distance, allowing Kevin to proceed at his own pace. After all, diaper-changing wasn't major surgery. Like a pro, Kevin had the baby cleaned and rediapered in a matter of moments, and all the while Carly simply stared at him, smiling.

Leah couldn't suppress her own smile, or the urge to applaud. "Good job. And now that you've passed that test, the big one comes a little later."

"Are you going to grade me on bottle preparation?"

"No. You're going to give your daughter a bath."

Kevin looked back at her and frowned. "How hard could that be?"

CHAPTER FIVE

BABIES SHOULDN'T only come with manuals, they should also come with handles. Kevin made that decision once he realized his soaked, squirming daughter would eventually have to come out of the water. Luckily, the tub Leah had brought fitted securely in the kitchen sink, which meant he didn't have to grab her from a kneeling position. That didn't make the task any less daunting. "What if I drop her?" This coming from a guy who played wide receiver in his high-school football tenure. Man, he needed to get a grip. Literally.

Leah opened a pink towel against her chest. "You won't drop her. Just hold her securely like I showed you, and then hand her to me. It's not that difficult."

Carly grinned as though she was enjoying his predicament. But then she'd been grinning at him since she'd arrived. That smile had more value than any journalism award. "Okay. Here goes, kiddo. Try not to move too much."

Slowly he clasped Carly by the waist, carefully lifted her up and handed her off to Leah before one drop of water reached the tile floor.

"That wasn't so bad, was it?" Leah asked.

Bad, no. Scary, yeah. Not that he would admit just how anxious he'd been. "Piece of cake."

Leah bundled Carly up into a tight towel cocoon. "I know it's unnerving, but you'll get the hang of it."

Damn, if she hadn't read his mind. "I guess so, but someone ought to develop some sort of lifting device, just in case." Or the aforementioned handles.

"I'll be sure to do that in my spare time. Right now I need to get Carly ready for bed," she called out as she walked from the kitchen and into the hallway.

Kevin followed her into the nursery, and once there, Leah laid the baby in the crib and grabbed a diaper and powder from the armoire before returning to the baby. "You're going to have to find her night clothes. They're in a blue suitcase somewhere in my bedroom. I should've unpacked instead of napping with your daughter."

Kevin had insisted she take that nap on the daybed in the nursery. In another time and place, he would've asked her to nap with him, minus the nap. "You needed some rest. Besides, you don't have to find any clothes for her tonight."

Leah looked appalled. "I'm not going to put her to bed in just a diaper."

"That's not what I meant." He crossed the room and opened the top drawer in the bureau to reveal several outfits in every imaginable color. "Mallory gave me some of the girls' baby clothes and she helped me buy a few things. It's all been washed."

"That was incredibly nice of Mallory."

"She enjoyed it." He rummaged around and after he found one particular item, he turned and held it up. "I picked this one out myself."

Leah hinted at a smile as she read the words embroidered across the front of the pink sleeper. "'Daddy's Girl.' Very sweet."

"It was either this or a mini football jersey, but I couldn't find one small enough. I'll get her one eventually."

When Kevin tried to hand her the footed pajamas, Leah wagged a finger at him. "I'm not going to dress her. You are."

The dressing part didn't seem so intimidating compared to the bath. But then he had to admit all the snaps looked confusing. "Okay, but don't blame me if I put it on backward."

When Leah moved aside, Kevin unfolded the towel encasing Carly and applied the diaper with ease. Now came the hard part.

"Feet first," Leah said before Kevin had time to figure out the mechanics.

He managed to get her legs into the sleeper but he wasn't sure how he was going to deal with the rest. "I'm not going to hurt her when I put her arms in it, am I?"

"Just take one arm at a time."

Kevin was surprised that it wasn't as difficult as it looked. Of course, Carly was totally cooperative, as though she'd done this before. Probably because she had. After he had the garment in place, he went to work on the snap maze that ran up one leg and all the way to her neck. He only missed a couple at first but before long, he had his daughter dressed. "All set, kiddo. You did good."

"So did you," Leah said, her smile fully formed.

"Thanks. I hope I'll get faster with practice. What now?"

"You can feed her if you'd like."

Kevin looked down at his chest and then back up again. "In case you haven't noticed, I'm not exactly equipped for that."

A touch of sadness crossed Leah's face. "I stopped breast-feeding this past week. I rarely found the time to pump while I was at work and my milk production was basically next to nothing. She's on formula now, and I hate that." Her tone indicated exactly how much she hated it.

When Leah glanced away, Kevin asked, "When a new mother comes to you with the same predicament, how do you respond?"

She sighed. "I tell her that the breast is best, but formula is a healthy alternative if it doesn't work out."

"Do you tell them they should feel guilty?"

"Of course not."

"Then you need to practice what you preach. You gave her that all-important colostrum, and you hung in there a lot longer than a lot of women with your schedule would have, so don't beat yourself up over it."

"How do you know about colostrum?"

"I've read up on it and a lot of other baby-rearing aspects."

Finally, her smile returned. "Have you ever given a baby a bottle before?"

"No, but I'm a quick study."

"I'll be right back."

After Leah left, Kevin gathered Carly into his arms, stood, and sat in the padded rocker across the room. She studied his face a moment before lifting her fist and bopping him twice in the chin. "Okay, I probably deserved that for a number of things, including not being there the day you were born."

She smiled as if to say, *That's okay, Dad. You're excused.* He bent and kissed her forehead, drawing in the scent of the lavender baby shampoo that had soothing properties, according to Leah.

He saw very little of his Irish father in Carly and a whole lot of his Armenian mother, right down to her dark eyes and hair. But then he, too, was a chip right off Lucine O'Brien's genetic block. And he couldn't discount Leah's Venezuelan heritage on her great-grandfather's side, either.

He continued to marvel at his daughter's features and recognized that every new dad most likely felt the way he did—that their kid was flawless. But as far as he was concerned, Carly was the portrait of perfection. Perfect face. Perfect hands. Perfect sweet disposition.

Without warning, Carly screwed up her face, stuck out her bottom lip and let out a scream that could rival a car alarm. Feeling helpless, Kevin held her against his shoulder and rocked the chair rapidly, patting her back. And when that didn't work, he got up and paced the room.

Thankfully, he saw Leah appear, bottle in hand, and saying, "That's her hungry cry."

"I gathered that," Kevin replied as he took the bottle and sat back down in the rocker.

Miraculously, the minute he stuck the nipple in Carly's mouth, she fell silent, aside from some serious sucking sounds. Yeah, she was definitely hungry.

Leah hovered above them, watching Kevin's every move. "Make sure you keep the bottle tilted up so she doesn't get much air in her tummy. A gassy baby is not a happy baby."

"Am I doing it right?" he asked.

"Yes, you are."

"Do you plan to watch me until she's done?"

"I do."

Talk about the consummate mother hen. "I promise I'm not going to screw this up, so in the meantime, why don't you go put the whirlpool to good use?"

"I don't think that's such a great idea."

Frustration hit him full-force. "Listen, Leah, I supervise ten junior reporters and I have a master's in journalism. I've even rebuilt a transmission and I made my mother a curio cabinet in high-school shop class. I'm capable of giving a baby a bottle on my own without—"

"I meant I'm not sure taking a bath is a great idea. I might never want to get out."

Okay, so he'd engaged in some severe conclusion-jumping. But in light of her attitude, and lack of trust in him, who could blame him? "If you're not out in thirty minutes, I'll check on you."

"That won't be necessary." Leah bent and kissed Carly's forehead. "I'll be back in twenty." When she looked down at where her palm rested on Kevin's forearm, she jerked her hand away, as though she'd touched a radiator.

Her reaction prompted Kevin to say, "It's going to happen."

She pulled her arms tightly around her middle. "I don't know what you mean."

"We're going to touch each other every now and then, even if it's only when we hand the baby to each other. You don't have to make such a big deal of it and act like I have some communicable disease."

"I'm not making a big deal of it, and I won't, as long as you understand that's the only touching we'll be doing."

She sounded to Kevin as if she might be trying to convince herself. "Understood."

She hooked a thumb over her shoulder. "I'm going to take my bath now. Again, I won't be long."

"Take your time. The towels are in the linen closet and Mallory stocked the shelf with aromatherapy stuff. Use whatever you'd like."

She began backing to the door. "Be sure to burp Carly after she's finished. I'll be back in time to put her to bed."

Once Leah had left the room, Kevin regarded Carly, who had already drained almost half the bottle. She paused long enough to smile at him.

"What's so funny, kiddo? Me giving you a bottle or your mom putting me in my place?"

She reached up again and this time tweaked his nose. He took her hand and kissed it softly, watching as her eyes closed briefly and slowly opened again.

Several times he'd heard his siblings talk about the joys of parenthood, but he'd never given it much thought until now. He never would've believed that holding a baby would be so satisfying. That he could feel such strong emotions for a child he'd only recently met. At least now he understood why his sister was such a daddy's girl.

Damn, if he hadn't become a certified sap. But that was okay. He'd trade all his machismo for these moments with Carly, and enjoy them while he still had the chance—before her mother took her away for good.

SHE'D SPENT way too much time in the bathtub. Dressed in the worn pink-cotton robe she'd owned since her freshman year of college, Leah wrapped her hair in a towel and hurried into the bedroom. She heaved one suitcase onto the mattress and rifled through it for something comfortable to wear, only to come across the animal-print pajamas Kevin had asked about during their phone conversation a week ago. And, like a practiced liar, she'd deceived him again. Although she'd intended to toss them during her packing, she couldn't bring herself to do it. Silly, considering she hadn't worn them since she and Kevin had called it quits. Correction. Since Kevin had quit on her. But then, she'd done some fairly inane things of late.

She remembered several memorable nights when

Kevin had taken them off her, slowly. Nights when he had taken her beyond the limits of lovemaking, using his hands and his mouth and his body. She shivered just thinking about the way he'd spoken to her in that deadly low and patently sexy voice of his. How easily he could draw every ounce of pleasure out of her until she thought she had nothing left, only to have him lead her right back into a sexual realm she'd never known existed....

"Did you enjoy yourself?"

At the sound of his voice, Leah whipped around toward the door, clutching the presumably trashed lingerie behind her back. Kevin stood in the open space, one arm braced on the frame, the other dangling at his side. He looked so imposing, so gorgeous, she wanted to shield her eyes before she did or said something stupid. "You might try knocking next time."

"Kind of hard when the door's open."

She wasn't particularly fond of his logic, or her lack thereof. "I was listening for the baby. By the way, where is she?"

He streaked a hand over his whisker-rough jaw. "She found my keys and went for a joyride. I tried to stop her but she's faster than she looks."

She wasn't fond of his attempt at humor, either. "Could you be serious for just a moment?"

He slid his hands into his jeans pockets and attempted to look contrite. "She fell asleep so I put her to bed."

"Just like that?"

"Yeah, just like that."

Amazing. "Did you put her on her back?"

"Yes, I did. Like I told you, I've read the books."

He was trying hard to impress her, and he was doing a fairly credible job. "Just remember, she rarely stays down the first time you put her down." Otherwise, Leah might be upset over not having the opportunity to say good-night to her daughter. "I'll go check."

"I would've heard her if she wasn't still asleep, and so would you." He pointed toward the nightstand and a silver object resembling a remote control set next to the alarm clock. "That's a wireless monitor. I have one in my room, too. The receiver's in the nursery. It's portable so you can carry it with you."

Evidently he'd thought of everything. "Great. That will come in handy. Now do you mind leaving so I can get dressed?"

"Sure, just as soon as you tell me what you're hiding behind your back."

"None of your business." Infuriating, nosy man.

He took a step toward her. "Did you buy me a gift?"

She took a step back. "No, I did not."

"If it's your panties, I've seen them before. Many times." He inclined his head and leaned forward. "But that's not what you're keeping from me, is it?"

Before Leah could react, he was on her like a moth on a porch light, grabbing for the pajamas. She managed to play keep-away by sidestepping out of his reach, but he didn't let up. She retreated and he stalked her until he had her backed up to the bed. The same bed where they had made long hot love more times than she could count. Dangerous, dangerous territory.

Everything seemed to come to a standstill except the rapid beat of Leah's heart. He was so close she could reach up and trace the line of his lips. Better still, she could kiss him. She could once more experience Kevin's thoroughly gifted mouth. When his gaze drifted to her lips, wisdom won out, causing Leah to concede that if she didn't give in and let him see the pajamas, she could be giving in to something much more unwise.

She held up the silk garment for his inspection. "Are you happy now?"

He had the gall to grin. "I thought you tossed those out."

She balled them up, dropped them onto the bed, then moved around him and away from his overwhelming magnetism. "I thought I'd gotten rid of them. I discovered I was mistaken when I started packing my clothes."

He sported a totally cynical look. "I didn't think you'd throw them away. They've always been your favorite."

She tightened the sash on her robe. "They were *your* favorite, not mine."

"I won't argue that, but I liked taking them off you, too."

Darned if that didn't make her quiver all over. "I've warned you about this kind of talk, Kevin."

"Sorry. I'm just being honest."

Leah pointed toward the door. "Please leave before I…" The power of his gaze stole the last remaining shred of coherency from her brain.

"Before you what?" he asked.

Before she did something that qualified as too stupid to live. "Please go so I can get dressed and then go check on my child. Be sure to close the door behind you."

He shrugged. "Fine, I'll meet you in the hall and we'll check on *our* child together."

After he left, Leah collapsed back on the bed and blew out a long breath. If she didn't get her head and hormones on straight, she'd find herself in the same predicament with a man she'd often found too hard to resist. This time, she *would* resist him, even if it meant avoiding him whenever possible. Unfortunately, he wasn't easy to ignore.

IF HE DIDN'T keep his mouth shut and his hands to himself, Kevin was in danger of driving Leah away before she even had a chance to settle in. He'd have to remind himself frequently that she'd agreed to the arrangement for the sake of convenience, and that she had a boyfriend. He didn't like it, but he couldn't do a damn thing about it. Or he wouldn't. At one time, he might have tried, but not now. Not if he wanted to prove to Leah that he still had a scrap of honor left.

Yet all his good intentions began to wane when Leah came out of the bedroom wearing a white T-shirt and an old pair of faded jeans with a strategic rip at the thigh.

A series of chants went off in his brain. He had to be strong. He had to ignore the urge to run his finger along that tear. He had to forget backing up her against the wall and…

"Is she still asleep?" she asked as soon as she reached him.

"I haven't heard a word out of her, but we can confirm that together."

Kevin pushed open the partially ajar door, allowing a stream of light from the hallway to spill into the room, illuminating the crib. With Leah by his side, they quietly made their way to the crib to find Carly lying motionless, her eyes fluttering slightly beneath closed lids.

Leah placed two fingers against her own lips then pressed them to the baby's cheek. He wanted to say, *Look what we've made, Leah,* but remained quiet until they left the room and reentered the hall.

Kevin wasn't ready to tell her good night, and that led to him spontaneously asking, "Do you want some wine?" although he fully expected a refusal.

"That sounds good," Leah answered, surprising the hell out of him. "As long as it's just one glass. I do have to work in the morning."

Silently they made their way into the kitchen, where Kevin retrieved a bottle of chardonnay—Leah's favorite—from the refrigerator. He popped the cork, poured two glasses and offered her one. "Let's take it onto the deck."

She frowned. "What if Carly wakes up?"

He pulled the monitor from his back pocket. "This has enough range to carry outside. We'll be able to hear her."

"Okay, I guess. As long as I can get to her quickly if she needs me."

Kevin could already tell Leah was going to err on the side of being overprotective, much like his own mother. But since Carly was Leah's first, he could understand her attitude to a point and opted to cut her some slack. He had to admit, he wasn't innocent when it came to worrying about his daughter. But he wasn't going to smother her, either.

When they walked onto the deck, Kevin pulled out a chair for Leah at the patio table and took the seat opposite her. The night was clear and relatively quiet with the exception of a chorus of locusts and the occasional passing car.

They both remained silent for a time before Leah said, "I love the smell of freshly mown grass. I love summer, period."

"I remember." And he did. Many times she'd mentioned she would take hot weather over cold any day. "We used to talk a lot about your fondness for the beach. We talked about a lot of things."

She released a humorless laugh. "Oh, sure. Aside from the weather, most of our conversations consisted of what sports superstar you'd interviewed and I'd issue a few complaints about my schedule, then we'd go to bed."

A direct attempt to depersonalize their former relationship, Kevin realized. "That's not true. We used to have lengthy conversations over dinner."

"*Then* we'd go to your apartment and go to bed. In fact, during the eight months we were involved, I don't remember one time when we were together when we didn't make love."

Yeah, and what a chore that had been. Not. "And your point?"

"I'm just saying we never developed a solid friendship."

"You're wrong, Leah. I valued your friendship almost as much as I appreciated you as a lover."

She pushed her glass aside and slid one hand through her damp hair. "I beg to differ. I still don't know everything about you, Kevin, and what I do know I practically had to drag out of you. Specifically your problems with Kieran."

That much was true, but then he hadn't wanted Leah to know all the questionable aspects of his past. "I did eventually tell you the details of why the relationship broke down."

"I know. He'd never liked the way you've lived your life and you didn't appreciate his tendency to judge you. But you haven't told me how and why you've settled your differences."

Now would be a good time to reveal the truth, but he couldn't force himself to do it. He didn't want to face her wrath over his dishonesty while they were rebuilding a relationship. A friendly relationship. "We reconnected about six months ago, not long after he met Erica, his fiancée." A good segue into a subject change. "By the way, Kieran's going to be a dad, too. Erica has an eleven-year-old daughter named Stormy. According to Kieran, that name fits her personality."

Leah smiled. "Nothing like jumping into fatherhood with a preteen female."

"A preteen female who was born with a heart condition," Kevin added. "But Stormy's okay now. In fact, she's one heck of a good softball player. And that reminds me of something. I'll be right back."

Kevin pushed away from the table and sprinted through the double doors and into the den housing his trophies. He opened one cabinet, retrieved the gift for his daughter, and returned to Leah.

He reclaimed his seat and laid the glove on the table. "I want Carly to have this. It's signed by a member of the U.S. Olympic softball team."

Leah picked up the mitt and inspected it. "Don't you think it's a little premature to be planning her softball career? She's still five years away from T-ball."

Kevin shook his head. "She's going to be too good to play T-ball. I'll have her ready to join the big girls' team by the time she's four. I'm thinking first base."

Another span of silence passed before she sighed.

"What is it?" he asked, curious about her mood and worried she might completely close down and close him out.

"I was thinking how lucky we are that Carly's healthy."

He wished he hadn't brought up his soon-to-be niece's condition. "Like I told you, Stormy's doing great."

"I'm glad she is, but I'm referring to all the kids I've treated who aren't okay."

He'd never seen her quite so pensive about her work. Maybe becoming a mother had something to do with that. "At least you're capable of helping those kids."

"Not all of them, Kevin. You'd be surprised at how many children have serious and oftentimes life-threatening diagnoses. Some are even the same age as Carly. It's not fair."

Now he wished he had whisky instead of wine. He didn't like medical talk in the least, but he felt compelled to listen to her since she needed to talk. Needed a friend. "No, it's not fair at all, but that's the way life goes. It can be a real crapshoot, whether we like it or not."

"But I really hate…" He words faded away along with her gaze.

"Hate what, Leah?"

She leaned forward and rimmed the edge of the glass with a fingertip. "You can't even imagine that moment after you discover a child might not survive an illness that you've diagnosed."

He didn't have to imagine it; he'd been in that moment as a patient on the receiving end of bad news. "I hate that you have to go through that, sweetheart." Her gaze snapped to his over the endearment, but he ignored it and continued. "I realize it's not easy for you. And anytime you have to face it while you're here, talk to me about it."

Her smile was tentative, but at least it was still a smile. "You're really serious about being friends?"

"I am."

"I guess only time will tell how well you handle that."

He planned to handle it well, no matter what it took. "Do you want a little more wine?"

She picked up her glass then stood. "Friends don't let friends drink too much when they have to work in the morning."

Kevin pushed his chair back and came to his feet. "You're right, and I'll take care of Carly when she wakes up again."

"We'll see who gets there first."

Then Leah did something Kevin hadn't come close to expecting. She walked right up to him, put her arms around his waist, kissed his cheek and said, "Thanks for listening, and thanks for everything."

Kevin couldn't help but believe that Leah was bent on testing him. And if she held on for any length of time, he'd probably fail. Mercifully, she stepped back, looking a little embarrassed and maybe even surprised that he hadn't put any moves on her. Truth was, he'd wanted more than just a friendly hug. More than just a polite thanks. He wanted her. Badly.

When he had enough presence of mind to speak, Kevin replied, "You're welcome. I'm glad you decided to move in."

"You know something? I'm glad too. I'll see you in the morning."

Yeah, she would, and he'd go to bed alone wondering what would have happened if he had taken the chance and kissed her. She probably would've slugged him first, and then asked questions later.

He gave himself a mental back-pat for controlling himself and meeting the challenge…this time.

CHAPTER SIX

WHEN THE ALARM shrilled like a sonic boom in Leah's ears, she rolled to her side and fumbled for the off button. And when she focused well enough to see the time, she shot out of bed like a missile.

After grabbing her robe from the club chair in the corner, she shrugged it on and headed straight for the nursery and found only an empty crib and no sign of Kevin or Carly. The smell of fresh-brewed coffee sent her toward the kitchen where she came upon a scene right out of a home movie. Kevin was seated at the dinette wearing a pair of navy-blue pajama bottoms, sans shirt, his hair mussed and his jaw shaded with a layer of whiskers. He had his bare feet propped on a chair and their daughter leaning back against his chest, his right arm wrapped securely around her middle and a newspaper clutched in his left hand.

Fortunately for Kevin, the sight served to temper some of Leah's irritation over not being woken to tend to her daughter. "Good morning, you two."

He glanced up at her and said, "Mornin'" in a raspy voice that Leah could listen to all day if she dared. That voice and his bare chest were almost too much for her to endure so early in the day, or anytime, for that matter. She should never have hugged him last night. That little faux pas had led to a few inadvisable thoughts that had kept her from readily falling asleep.

"It seems the monitor isn't working," she said, her tone hinting at displeasure directed at both him and herself.

"It works if you turn it on."

Her dismay increased. "Why didn't you tell me it wasn't on?"

Kevin turned the page without looking at her. "Because you needed to sleep."

"I needed to be able to hear my child when she woke up."

He planted a kiss on the crown of Carly's head. "Oh, she woke up all right. Twice in fact. But we managed just fine. I gave her a bottle the first time, and the second time, about an hour ago, we came in here to see what's up in the world of sports."

When Carly kicked at the paper, Kevin smiled at her and said, "I know what you mean, baby girl. He's not worth the size of that contract. His ERA isn't that great, and he won't help the team all that much if they make it to the playoffs. And that's a big if."

Both Carly and Kevin seemed totally disinterested in Leah, which only heightened her exasperation. "Kevin, could you put the paper down a minute and talk to me?"

He afforded her only a passing glance. "Sure, but

why don't you have some coffee? It might improve your mood."

"My mood is fine." She advanced to the table, kissed Carly's cheek and almost did the same to Kevin. It was as if some past instinct to do that very thing had been seared into her psyche.

It's morning and Kevin needs a kiss.

Before she could act on the urge, Leah made her way to the coffeemaker and poured some of the brew into a mug set out on the counter. As usual, she nixed cream and sugar, a habit she'd acquired during medical school.

She leaned back against the counter and watched father and daughter bonding as Kevin listed the baseball all-star selections. And Carly, as if she knew what he was saying, looked completely engrossed.

"You should've woken me up," Leah said, feeling somewhat more coherent and a bit less angry over Kevin usurping her duties. After all, he meant well, and she couldn't remember a time when she'd slept all night, uninterrupted.

Kevin set the paper aside and shifted Carly to his shoulder. "Like I said, you needed to sleep, and I handled everything fine. Her diaper's on straight and her belly's full. I even refused to let her watch cable when she begged me." He followed the comment with a rapid-fire grin.

"Very cute." And so was Kevin. *Very* cute.

Leah glanced at the clock on the kitchen stove and realized how little time she had to get ready for work.

"Since it's getting late, I'd appreciate it if you'd watch her while I get dressed."

"Not a problem at all. We still need to cover the west-coast standings."

"I also need to pack her bag for day care."

"Done."

Leah's mouth fell open before she snapped it shut again. "How would you know what she needs?"

He nodded toward the yellow bag set out on the counter. "I found your list. Bottles, diapers, wipes and two extra outfits. Feel free to check it out."

She was having enough trouble checking him out, particularly his noteworthy chest and that little brush-stroke of hair at his sternum, well-known territory that she'd explored willingly at one time, and often. "I trust you, as long as you followed the list."

After Carly started to fuss, Kevin rose from the chair and began to walk around the room. "Do you trust me enough to pick her up early so I can take her to my parents' house?"

That would entail putting Carly in the car with Kevin, and although he'd always been a good driver, he did like to speed at times. "Do you promise to drive safely and slowly?"

"I'll be sure not to drag race on the Interstate."

"I'm being serious, Kevin."

"No kidding," he muttered.

Agreeing to his request also meant leaving their child completely in his care. Then again, his mother had raised six kids and knew what she was doing. At least he'd have reinforcements if he encountered any problems with the baby. "What time are you suggesting you pick her up?"

He paused his pacing. "Around three. I want to beat rush-hour traffic."

"And you'll be back when?"

He took his former place at the table, turned Carly back around and bounced her gently on his lap. "I'll be home around six at the latest, maybe earlier, depending how it goes with the folks."

"Do you honestly expect trouble?"

"Not really. I figure once they see her, they aren't going to be angry at me for not saying something sooner."

"Fine. I'm sure you'll both have a great time."

Since Leah had hospital rounds this evening, he could very well beat her home. For some strange reason, she was a little miffed that he hadn't asked her to join them. Perhaps even a little hurt.

As if he'd read her mind, Kevin added, "I'd ask you to stop by, but I think it's better if I kind of ease them into the whole idea of me being a father."

"That's okay. I'm not family." At one time she'd hoped to be. "But I would like to meet them before I move."

Kevin's demeanor suddenly went from pleasant to serious. "I'm sure that can be arranged."

"We'll talk about it later. Right now I need to hurry. I'll put out some clothes for Carly if you don't mind getting her dressed."

"I don't mind, and I'm capable of picking out her clothes myself."

Now he sounded just plain crabby. "I'm sorry. This is going to take some getting used to, you playing Dad."

"I'm not playing, Leah. I am her dad."

How well she knew that. Just seeing Carly in his arms served as a constant reminder. "Yes, you are." She felt the need to dole out a little benevolence. "And you're doing a good job so far."

He appeared genuinely pleased by the compliment. "Thanks. Let's hope my parents feel the same."

KEVIN HAD a solid grip on the safety seat containing a snoozing baby and a strong feeling he should have called first. But he was already standing on the porch of his childhood home, prepared to introduce the newest grandchild to the—he hoped—proud grandparents.

After he rang the bell, the heavy sound of footsteps provided Kevin with some relief. His dad was about to answer the summons and his legendary sense of humor could help to diffuse the situation. Kevin predicted that his mother was going to be exceedingly ticked off over the fact he hadn't told her about the baby before now.

The door creaked opened, revealing Dermot O'Brien, the hulking, sandy-haired Irish patriarch who'd spent most of Kevin's formative years entertaining his friends, girls and guys alike.

"Well, I'll be," he said. "Our wayward son has come to visit." When Dermot noticed Carly, he centered his gaze on Kevin, but he didn't appear to be all that shocked. "Now if you would be tryin' to leave that wee one on our doorstep, I'm sorry, boyo. I've already raised six of them and I'm too old to raise more."

"Nope, Dad. She's a keeper, and that's what I intend to do. Keep her."

Kevin expected to see the cogs of confusion turning in his dad's head but that, remarkably, didn't happen. "I'm thinkin' you have quite a bit of explaining to do to your ma," he said as he stepped aside.

"You could say that," Kevin murmured as he walked into the modest den, still decorated much the same as it had been when he'd left home some seventeen years ago, right down to the same floral sofa and chair.

After setting the car seat on the couch, he faced his father and asked, "Where is Mom?"

"Fixing a bit of supper." Dermot turned toward the kitchen and bellowed, "Lucy, my love, your boy is here."

"Which boy?"

"Kevin."

"Wonderful! I'll be right there."

A split second later, Lucine O'Brien came rushing out of the kitchen, her salt-and-pepper dark hair pulled back in a low bun. She wiped her hands on her apron and drew Kevin into a mama-bear hug that belied her small stature. "It's so good to see you, dear. I'm making that chicken dish you've always loved. Can you stay for dinner?"

After he pulled the explanation train into revelation central, she might withdraw the invite. "Is it the chicken with the noodles?"

"Yes, it is. I've also made peach cobbler."

Oddly, she still hadn't noticed the baby. "Sounds great, Mom."

When his dad cleared his throat, his mom asked, "Did you need something, Dermot?"

"No, my love. I just thought you should know that your boy brought you a gift, although it's not original. I gave you the same thing six times."

Lucy frowned. "What are you talking about, old man?"

His dad nodded toward Carly, who was awake and looking around the room. Kevin walked to the baby, unhooked the harness, lifted her up and turned her around in his arms. "Mom, Dad, this is Carly, my daughter."

If Kevin had had a toy basketball handy, he could have dropped a three-pointer into his mother's mouth. "I don't understand, Kevin."

Which meant she understood what he was saying, just not why he hadn't said it sooner. "I didn't know about her until recently."

Without saying a word, Lucy took Carly into her arms and looked at her with awe. "I've hoped for so long that you would settle down, Kevin. I knew in my heart it would happen, but I never dreamed you would have a child."

His transformation had begun the minute he'd received a possible death sentence. The baby had only cemented his resolve to straighten out his life. "I never thought I'd have a child, either, but she's mine."

Lucy tore her gaze from Carly and landed it on Kevin. "Who's the mother?"

He'd expected the question and had tried to come up

with a reasonable explanation. "Her name's Leah Cordero. She's a pediatrician. You'd like her."

Lucy suddenly handed the baby over to Dermot. "Kevin, I could use your help getting a platter down from the cabinet."

His mother didn't need his help. She wanted to get him alone so she could grill him. Kevin looked at his dad, who'd taken a seat in his favorite lounger and was holding Carly up above his head while making ridiculous faces at her.

"Be careful with her, Dermot," his mother scolded. "You're going to hurt her."

"I've done this before, Lucine."

And this was exactly the problem Kevin had with his mom—her tendency to be overprotective to a fault. "She's fine, Mother. She's not going to break."

Without responding, Lucy walked away. And Kevin, like the dutiful son, trailed after her even knowing he probably wasn't going to care for what she had to say.

When she donned her concerned face the minute they reached the kitchen, Kevin leaned back against the counter and waited for the lecture. He didn't have to wait long.

"Are you going to marry this Leah?"

"No, Mom. She's going to be leaving at the end of August and setting up her practice in Mississippi."

"And you're going to just let her walk away with your child?"

He didn't like it any more than she did. "I'll see Carly when I can."

Lucy shook her head. "Do you realize the importance of raising a child in a two-parent home?"

"I don't have a choice, Mom. Leah's seeing another man." No matter how many times he'd said that, he still wanted to choke on the words.

She began lining up a series of vegetables on the counter. "Even worse, another man raising your daughter. What do you know about him?"

Not much. "Leah has good judgment. I'm just going to have to trust her. And she's going to have to learn to trust me with Carly."

"Well, at least she believes you can take care of the baby, otherwise you wouldn't be here with her."

"Actually, I'm planning on taking care of her all day while Leah's at work, at least until she moves." As soon as he'd convinced Leah he could deal with an infant.

Lucy's expression brightened. "Wonderful, dear. I'll clear my schedule and help you. We'll have such fun."

"I don't need any help, Mother." When her elation faded, Kevin added, "It's important to me to do this by myself."

His mother looked unconvinced. "You've barely recovered from your illness, Kevin. It would be no trouble for me to help you."

He could understand why she might think him incapable of caring for an infant, even though she would never come right out and say it. "It's been six months since the procedure, Mom. I appreciate your offer, but I can manage taking care of Carly."

Lucy laid a hand on his arm. "You have no idea what it's like, Kevin, taking care of a baby. There's so much to worry about."

"You're right. I'm going to worry about Carly, but I'm not going to suffocate her. I want her to grow up strong and independent."

He could tell from the mist forming in her eyes that he'd wounded her with his careless words.

Kevin came up behind her and gave her a hug. "I'm sorry, Mom. I didn't mean to make you cry."

"I always cry when I'm chopping onions."

"You're cutting up a tomato."

She waved him away. "You need to go see about your daughter, unless you want her first word to be an Irish insult."

She had a point, and he had one small way to make it up to her. "Set a place for me. I'll stay for dinner."

She attempted a slight smile. "Good. Now hurry along so I can finish up."

Kevin returned to the den, only to find it deserted. He couldn't imagine where his father had gone with his daughter, until he glanced at the sliding glass doors and found the pair seated on the covered patio. Carly looked content in her grandfather's lap, waving her arms like an orchestra conductor.

Kevin walked outside, pulled up a lawn chair and joined them. "It's kind of hot out here. I think I should take her back inside before she gets overheated." And now he sounded just like his mother.

"There's plenty of shade," Dermot said. "And this

little lassie is made of solid Irish stock, although I'm thinkin' your mother's Armenian roots overtook the Irish. She's not the least bit fair of skin."

His dad had always put a lot of importance on cultural lineage, particularly the Irish part. "Leah's great-grandfather was Venezuelan, so that accounts for some of her darker coloring."

Dermot bounced the baby a couple of times. "Then she is a little melting pot, she is." He took his attention from the baby and gave Kevin a curious look. "Did your ma give you a hard time, son?"

"Not too bad. She'd be happier if I told her I was going to marry Leah."

His father sat silent for a moment. "Did you tell her that you're livin' with the lass?"

Kevin swallowed hard around his shock. "How did you know about that?"

"I spoke with Kieran not long ago. We both decided it would be best if you told your ma yourself."

Great. His brother had ratted on him, just like in the old days. And his father had basically decided to keep the news to himself, in turn forcing Kevin to face the proverbial music alone. "At least that explains your initial reaction when I delivered the news. You didn't blink an eye."

"Your old da can keep a secret. And now I have a secret for you."

Kevin wasn't sure he could handle any more secrets. But out of respect, he said, "Go ahead."

Dermot's expression turned suddenly somber. "One

night, when you were in the hospital and they were feeding you that poison before you had the blood transplant, your ma had gone out for some coffee. She left me to sit with you, and you were so bloody sick it made my old heart hurt."

Kevin didn't care to relive the chemo process, although he still had occasional nightmares about being surrounded by masked faces while he was shackled to a bed with no means of escape. "I'm okay now, Dad."

"I know that, son. Now let me finish."

Kevin sat back and accepted his fate—more fatherly commentary. "All right."

"You were blatherin' words I couldn't understand," Dermot continued. "Then you opened your eyes and clear as a summer morn, you said, 'I'm sorry, Leah. I love you.' I knew right then you'd made a hames out of a relationship with some woman."

Yeah, he'd definitely made a mess out of the relationship. But he had to question the truth in his father's claim about the sick-bed confession. Not once had he told Leah he loved her, even though sometimes he thought he did feel that way about her. Correction. He was fairly sure he had. "I was talking out of my head, Dad."

"You were pining for her, son. I saw it in your eyes." His dad shifted Carly around to where she was facing Kevin. "Do you still have more than a fondness for this baby's mother?"

If he issued a denial, he'd be handing his father one major lie. "Yes, but—"

"Is she promised in marriage to the man she is seeing?"

Apparently his father knew the entire story, thanks to Kieran. "Not that I'm aware of."

"Then it's not too late for you to win back her heart, laddie."

At one time, Kevin might have considered doing that very thing, boyfriend or no boyfriend. That was before he'd made a concerted effort to change his ways instead of disregarding other people's feelings. "I'm surprised at you, Dad, suggesting I try to steal another man's woman."

Dermot raised an eyebrow. "Where is this man, Kevin? If your ma told me she was going to move in with some ape, there'd be wigs on the green. I'd be poundin' on his door, demanding my love leave his house. Then I would cold-cock him, I would."

"I'm not sure Leah's told her boyfriend about the living arrangement." In fact, the guy had never even called the house, which meant he was probably calling her cell phone. Or not calling at all. Purely wishful thinking on his part.

Dermot handed Carly over to Kevin, stretched his legs out before him and clasped his hands atop his belly. "If she has told the man, then he's a bollocks for not doin' a thing about it. And you would be a fool not to woo her. If her heart isn't ripe for the pickin', you will not be able to steal it. But if it is, you will know soon enough."

"I appreciate the suggestion, Dad." Even if he had no immediate goal that entailed putting any moves on Leah. At least that's what he'd planned.

"Just one more bit of advice, son." Dermot leaned

over and covered Carly's ears. "Keep your langer in your cacks and let the lass take the lead. She just might surprise you."

Kevin had to admit his father's advice was dead-on. He wasn't going to do anything to compromise his arrangement with Leah. But he greatly doubted she was going to surprise him, either.

LEAH ARRIVED HOME four hours late, completely exhausted, with aching feet and the beginnings of a headache. But her spirits lifted when she walked into the great room to discover Kevin lying on his back, eyes closed, with Carly resting atop his chest, her legs bunched beneath her and bottom sticking up in the air. She couldn't decide which sight was more endearing—this portrait of father and daughter sleeping, or coming upon Kevin reading the paper to Carly that morning.

As badly as she hated to disturb them, Leah needed to put the baby to bed. But before she disrupted the scene, she retrieved her cell phone and snapped a photo to capture the moment.

After dropping her phone back into her lab-coat pocket, Leah lifted the baby and carried her into the nursery. She carefully put her in the crib and halfway expected Carly to wake up bright-eyed and bushy-tailed from her late nap. Yet she didn't move an inch, or really stir, for that matter. It appeared the afternoon meeting with her grandparents had worn her out. Worn them both out, she decided when she returned to the great room to find Kevin still

sleeping. His slack features and steady respiration indicated he might be there for a while, if not all night.
Unless she woke him.

Nope. She'd let him sleep. And while he slept, she
would take the opportunity to steal a good look at
him. She took a visual journey over the white muscle
shirt showcasing his toned arms and from there she
moved on to the blue pajama bottoms covering his
slender hips, thinking it best not to linger there too
long. She even studied his bare feet that quite honestly
were nicer than most male feet, despite his slightly
crooked toes.

She centered her gaze on his hand now resting on
his abdomen. Leah absolutely loved his hands. Several
times she'd been content just sitting and watching those
long, masculine fingers play over the computer keyboard while he worked on an article for the magazine.
She also remembered being completely hypnotized
when he used those very skilled hands on her.

Leah blamed the full-body shiver on the air-condi-
tioning vent blowing cold air down from above her. She
considered covering Kevin with the throw draped over
the sofa's arm, but then again, he'd always been hot-
blooded. So hot-blooded that he refused to sleep
beneath the covers when they'd been in bed. In fact, he
refused to sleep in anything at all. And that was one
image she needed to exile from her mind.

As Leah reached for the near-empty baby bottle on
the coffee table, the same hand she'd been admiring
only moments before snaked out and grabbed her wrist,

followed by a blatantly sensual voice declaring, "Hey, I'm not done with that yet."

Leah inadvertently tipped over the bottle and caught it before it rolled to the floor, in turn dislodging Kevin's grasp.

"Sorry," he said. "I didn't mean to scare you."

"Well, you did." She held up the bottle and inspected it. "Funny, this looks like formula, not beer."

Kevin draped his long legs over the sofa and sat up. "I don't touch the stuff anymore. Beer or formula."

Leah had never considered Kevin a hard-core drinker, but he had liked his ale. "Sure. And you don't watch baseball anymore, either."

"I'm serious. I've laid off the beer since I started working out more frequently."

She'd noticed the rewards from his new fitness regimen. "But you still drink wine."

He rose from the sofa and rubbed a hand over his nape. "That wine we had last night was the first alcohol I've had in months."

Leah admittedly had a difficult time believing he'd given up partying hearty in her absence. But she was too tired to challenge him. "If you say so."

"It's true." Kevin looked around the room then back down on the couch. "By the way, where's the kid? Did she run off in the car again? I swear I hid my keys."

Leah couldn't suppress her smile. "I put her to bed, which is exactly where I intend to go."

"I'm going to work out for a while."

"You're going to the gym this late?"

"No. I'm going outside to the cabana. I have some cardio equipment and weights out there. Kieran set everything up for me as a housewarming gift."

"Very nice. I wouldn't mind using the equipment."

Kevin stretched his arms high above his head, causing the shirt to part from the band of his pajamas, and exposing his navel along with a glimpse of the path below that Leah used to trace with a fingertip, just so she could watch him writhe in anticipation. To hear him beg. To make him sweat. "My equipment is your equipment," he said as he dropped his arms. "Feel free to use it any time."

That conjured up all sorts of dubious thoughts in Leah's randy brain. "Thanks, but I'll have to pass tonight. I do need to make up a few more bottles before I go to bed."

"I've already done that," he said. "I also gave Carly her bath without fumbling her. Do I get a prize?"

Rewarding him in unconventional yet sexy ways momentarily entered Leah's mind. Instead, she handed him the bottle. "You could try washing this without fumbling it."

When he took the bottle from her, Leah could have sworn he brushed a fingertip across her wrist. Or maybe she'd just imagined it. Wished for it, even. "You must be starving," Kevin said.

Was she that obvious? "Why would you think that?"

"Because knowing you, you didn't stop long enough to have dinner. But that's okay. My mom sent a plate of food home with me. You're welcome to it."

Normally she wouldn't consider putting something in her stomach so late, but Kevin had been correct in his assumptions. She hadn't had a thing since lunch. She was also curious to learn about his parents' reaction to the baby. "I could eat a little something."

"Great."

Leah followed Kevin into the kitchen and stood by while he pulled a plastic-covered paper plate from the refrigerator and popped it into the microwave. He turned and leaned back against the counter. "How was your day?"

"Okay. And I'm sorry I'm so late. I had to admit two infants to the hospital because of some rampant summer virus going around."

"Will they be all right?" he asked with sincere concern.

Leah took a seat on a stool set out at the kitchen island. "They should both make a full recovery, barring any complications."

"Good." He pulled a fork and knife out of a drawer and laid them, along with a napkin, before her. "I have another question. What have you been doing with Carly when you've had to work late?"

"Fortunately, the day care's geared for medical personnel, so they run two shifts of workers, one for the day and another at night. I do have to pay extra for the nightly service if I need it."

"At least that's one less thing you have to worry about," he said. "As long as you're living here, I'm available 24/7."

"I really appreciate that. Now it's your turn to tell me how it went with your folks."

He grabbed a bottle of water from the refrigerator and handed it to Leah. "Better than I expected. My dad took the news in stride, but as I predicted, my mom was disappointed I hadn't told her sooner. She also wasn't too pleased when I refused her offer of help. I told her taking care of Carly was something I wanted to do myself."

Leah understood his attitude completely. Kevin had always been sensitive when it came to his mother's penchant for being overly helpful where he was concerned. "Did you make it clear that our living arrangement is only temporary?"

He studied the tiled floor. "I didn't exactly cover that subject."

A case of supreme avoidance. "She has no idea I'm living with you?"

"I decided I need to ease her into the idea. Learning about the baby was enough for one day." When the microwave dinged, Kevin opened the door, retrieved the plate and slid it in front of her. "Here's your dinner, Dr. Cordero. Enjoy."

She surveyed the pile of food. "I need to let it cool off a bit, but it looks good."

"Believe me, it is."

She picked up the fork and knife and cut a few pieces of chicken. "I've always envied people who have a way with food. Cooking isn't exactly my forte, either."

Kevin moved beside her and leaned a hip against the

island. "You could say that. I've never known anyone who could burn a pot of fettuccine."

Leah spun the stool to face him. "Hey, that's not fair. That was your fault."

He shrugged. "I didn't leave the pasta on the stove until all the water boiled out of it."

"No, but if I recall correctly, you distracted me. You'd just returned from a trip to New York, you stormed into my apartment and said, 'Step away from the stove, woman, and take off your clothes. Your daddy's back in town.'"

"That's not what I said."

"Maybe not verbatim, but—"

"Not even close." When he leaned toward her, Leah held her breath as he rested his lips against her ear and whispered, "I said 'I've missed you, baby, and I want to show you how much. Dinner can wait.'"

He moved back, but still remained very close. If Leah owned even a wisp of wisdom, she would avoid looking at his eyes, but she didn't. If she knew what was best, she wouldn't dare stand up and get closer to him, which she did. If she had any regard for self-preservation, she'd be crazy to even consider what she was tempted to do next.

But she was considering it. More than that, she was going to do it, shirk all her good sense for one moment of pleasure. A moment when she could take the memories and turn them into reality.

She needed the intimacy, regardless of the consequences, and it was going to happen. She couldn't stop it. She didn't want to.

CHAPTER SEVEN

HE COULD HANDLE a simple kiss. A closed-mouth, chaste, hey-we're-friends kiss. But an open-mouth, wicked, down-and-dirty kiss was just about more than Kevin could take.

If he didn't bring this mouth action to an end right away, he was in danger of carrying Leah straight into his bedroom without a second thought. If he didn't control his hands, which had somehow traveled to her butt, he might only manage to make it to the den. And if she didn't stop pressing her sweet little body against him, they just might have to get reacquainted on the kitchen island.

But he wasn't going to take her anywhere, and not because he didn't want to. If he made a wrong move, he'd be compromising good intentions, as well as his newfound honor. And yeah, it sucked. In a massive way.

With what little resistance he had left, Kevin broke all contact and took a much-needed step back. And while Leah stood in stunned silence, he rounded the island, putting a solid mass of granite and wood between them, in turn concealing the effect that incendiary kiss had had on his body.

He could barely catch a breath, but at least he'd kept his langer in his cacks. His dad would be so proud.

Leah braced her elbows on the island and momentarily covered her face before staring up at him. "I can't believe that just happened."

Kevin raised both of his hands, palms forward. "I didn't do it." He sounded like a college kid who'd been caught plagiarizing his mid-term paper.

"You should have said something to stop me."

"Kind of hard to talk when you have your tongue in my mouth. And it's real hard to think when you have your hands all over me."

"I know, I know." She slapped her palms on the counter and straightened. "I've done it twice now."

Twice? Had he missed something? "Unless we made out when I was in a coma, it's only happened once."

"I meant I've broken the rules twice. The kiss and talking about the past, which led to the kiss. If you hadn't started with that 'I've missed you, baby' story, then it wouldn't have happened."

"Oh, so now it's my fault."

"It's both our faults, and it won't happen again."

If Kevin had his way, it *would* happen again. Several times. A day. And night. "Remember, I'm the one who stopped it before it went any further. And you and I both know it would have gone further if I hadn't stopped."

She frowned. "The Kevin O'Brien I knew before wouldn't have stopped it. So why did you?"

"First of all, I'm not the same man you knew a year ago. Secondly, you didn't have a boyfriend back then." And that led to a question he'd wanted to ask for some time now. "That reminds me, why hasn't he called you?"

She failed to look at him when she said, "He only has my cell phone number, and we've both been busy."

Time for a little more necessary interrogation. "Exactly what does he do for a living?"

Her gaze came back to him. "Why do you ask?"

"Because I want to know a little bit about the man who could be raising my daughter in the future."

"He's a mechanic."

That was totally unanticipated. "Oh, yeah?"

"Is there a problem with that, Kevin?"

Kevin had only one problem with the guy—his involvement with Leah. "I don't have anything against mechanics. I've used them before. But didn't you say he owned his own business?"

She sighed. "Yes. Anything else you want to know? Maybe his political affiliation or his shoe size?"

He'd been waiting for the right moment to pose the most important question, and that moment had arrived. "Does he know you're living here?"

A flash of guilt passed over her expression. "No, but I plan to tell him soon. I just haven't had the chance."

Like he really believed that. "He's not going to be happy about it, is he?"

"He's not going to care. He trusts…" Her words faltered along with her gaze.

Kevin came upon an idea that could help. Help him figure out if he even liked the jerk. "If you want me to talk to him—"

"No!" The word echoed in the room like a gunshot.

"Fine. If he calls, I'll pretend I'm the gardener."

She pointed behind her. "I'm going to take a shower now."

"What about your food?"

"I'm not hungry."

"All signs point to the contrary. Or maybe I should say all mouths point to the contrary."

She hinted at a smile. "Shut up, Kevin."

"Okay, but first I have a request."

She gave him a wary look. "If you're going to ask me to—"

"It's about Carly. I want to start picking her up from the day care at noon, beginning tomorrow."

"You can pick up her at four."

Not good enough, as far as he was concerned. "One."

"Three."

"Deal."

Kevin was fairly surprised she hadn't put up more of a fight. Either she was too tired to argue, or she'd decided to compensate him for the kiss.

When a whimper sounded from the monitor set out on the counter near the stove, Leah said, "I haven't seen her all day, so I'll take care of her. Unless you insist on doing it."

Normally, he would. But if he moved from behind the island, he'd reveal exactly how hard it had been to halt that little round of tongue tango. "Go ahead. I'll take the next shift. Right now I'm going to stay here a few more minutes and calm down."

Finally, she smiled. "Oh, that."

"Yeah, *that.*"

And "that" could keep him awake most of the night.

PRETTY BOYS and their toys should be outlawed, Leah's first thought when she entered the cabana midmorning and found Kevin lifting weights. Since the bench was turned horizontally to her, he didn't notice she'd come into the room. And that gave her a few moments to engage in a little covert inspection.

She'd spent her medical training studying anatomy, not only that of children but also of men and women of all shapes and sizes. By now she should be unaffected by the human body. His human body. His very male, incredible human body.

Yet every sinewy muscle in his arms and legs exposed by the tank and shorts he wore, every prominent vein that showed when he raised the weights, every plane and angle of Kevin's anatomical framework captured her fancy. Even when he was sweating and hissing out short puffs of air with his effort.

She needed to say what she'd come to say before she found herself lost in a pheromone fog. She'd already walked into that trap last night. And even this morning, when she'd handed the baby over to him so she could shower, it took every ounce of strength not to investigate his mouth again.

Just when Leah was about to clear her throat to garner his attention, Kevin dropped the weight on the bar, slid down the bench, sat up and swung his legs over the side. When she moved forward into his field of vision, he looked blatantly surprised.

"What are you doing here?" he asked as he stood and swiped an arm across his damp forehead. "Did you forget something?"

She'd forgotten herself last night. She could have a memory lapse right now if she didn't stop staring at his rather well-toned thighs and an area not too far above those thighs. "Actually, I dropped Carly off at the day care and suddenly remembered we're getting low on formula. After I finished hospital rounds, I dropped by the store and brought it back." Only an excuse to return, and not a great one at that.

Clearly he saw through. "You could've called me instead of driving all the way back here."

"Okay, that's not the only reason I came home. I want to talk about what happened in the kitchen."

"The coffee wasn't that bad this morning. Maybe a little strong, but I've had worse." His grin was teasing and so was his tone.

"That's not what I'm referring to and you know it."

He pointed at a shelf to her left. "Could you hand me a towel?"

Rather than risk coming too close to him, Leah retrieved the white terry towel and tossed it at him. After it landed on the floor about two feet in front of him, he raked it off the tan ceramic tile and rubbed it slowly over his neck and the top of his chest. How much she wished she were that towel.

"As I was saying," she continued, "I need to explain my actions last night."

He draped the towel over the arm of the treadmill. "You don't have to explain anything, Leah. I know what's going on with you."

She must be as transparent as gauze. "Oh you do, do you?"

"Yeah. Your boyfriend's hundreds of miles away and you're on hormone overload. It happens."

He was so far off the mark it wasn't even funny. Except maybe for the hormone theory. "You have no idea what you're talking about."

"I know exactly what I'm talking about. When we were still together, for about three or four days out of the month, I couldn't come within a foot of you without you climbing all over me. It didn't matter where we were. In restaurants, you'd put your hand on my thigh underneath the table even knowing what you were doing to me a few inches above that. I remember one time in the movie theater when we had to leave because you got all hot and bothered over a love scene. We never even made it out of the parking lot before we got it on. Not that I'm complaining. I looked forward to those days."

"That's ridiculous." But true. When she ovulated, she turned into a rampant, horny she-cat. Actually, she had very few days during the month when she hadn't been like that around Kevin.

"Tell me something, Leah," he said in his sexy I-dare-you voice. "Does your boyfriend have the stamina to handle you on those days when you're so hot it takes hours to cool you down? Does he know precisely where to touch you and what to say to you to send you over the edge, like I do?"

A series of images from the past flashed in Leah's mind, blanketing her entire body in heat. "That's none of your business."

He had the audacity to try on an innocent look. "Just wondering."

"Well, you can quit wondering. I need to get back to work." Before she found herself in another precarious predicament. "Don't forget to pick up Carly this afternoon."

"Don't forget to put the formula next to the three cans I bought two days ago."

She pivoted and marched out the door, the sound of Kevin's laughter following her all the way back into the house where she made a decision to prevent resuming what she'd once had with Kevin—one rip-roaring sex life.

Maybe making the call wasn't such a hot idea, but Leah felt as if she had no other option. She strode down the hall, stepped into her bedroom, pulled out her cell from her pants pocket and hit the number on the speed dial. The phone rang five times and just when she was about to hang up, a gruff voice answered, "Camp's Automotive."

"Hey, J.W., it's Leah."

A long paused followed before he said, "It's good to hear from you, sweet britches, but I'm busier than a tailless donkey during mosquito season. Can I call you back?"

She hated the nickname he'd give her years ago, but she wasn't going to correct him now. "As a matter of fact, I want you to call me back. But I need to give you my new address and phone number."

"I didn't know you'd moved."

"As of last weekend. It's a long story." And that was all he needed to know at the moment. "I won't go into any details right now, but call me this evening on the home phone. I'll explain it all then."

"Will do. I have a couple of things I need to tell you, too."

"Do you have a pen and paper?"

"Right here."

Leah dictated the information and then said, "Remember, call me on the home phone. It's important."

"Got it. How's sweet-britches junior fairing? And didn't she turn four months old yesterday?"

Lord, Leah hadn't even remembered her own child's birthday. Some mother she was turning out to be. "Yes, she's officially four months old. And she's growing like a weed. You won't recognize her when we move back in August."

"Probably not. Give her a kiss from her Uncle J.W., okay?"

"I will. Now get back to work and we'll talk soon."

After she hung up, Leah pocketed the phone and instantly felt ashamed. The significant-other charade was getting out of hand, but she didn't feel as if she could make any revelations to Kevin. Especially not now. Not after that full-throttle kiss last night. Not after he'd admitted that the boyfriend factor had played a part in his ability to maintain control. Good thing he had retained that control because hers had nearly taken a cross-country hike in the cabana.

Admittedly, keeping up the deception until she departed could prove to be difficult. She feared she might eventually slip up. Maybe she should tape her mouth shut whenever she was around Kevin. That could be beneficial on two levels—she couldn't spill the beans or engage in more mouth-to-mouth with him.

That flaming kiss had been the bane of her existence, both last night and all morning long. But duty called and maybe that duty would assist her in putting Kevin and the kiss out of her mind.

AFTER SHE ARRIVED at the clinic, Leah approached the reception desk to take a look at the upcoming schedule, but made it only halfway before Kathy, one of the nurses, prevented her progress. "Dr. Cordero, I thought you might want to see this."

The way her day had been going, Leah wasn't exactly stunned that something was wrong. "What is it, Kathy?"

"It's the lab results for the Myesky boy."

Brandon Myesky—a rambunctious four-year-old

who could charm the entire medical staff with only a dimpled grin. Only, lately, the little boy hadn't been smiling at all, and Leah worried her worst fears were about to be realized. "How bad is it?"

"Most likely leukemia."

Even though she'd expected as much, the confirmation took a moment to register. "Are you sure?"

The woman opened a chart, turned it around and pointed at the lab slip. "It's right here."

After she scanned the results, nausea settled like a rock in Leah's stomach. "Are the Myeskys scheduled to come in soon?"

"I called them about an hour ago. They'll be here in about two hours. I asked them not to bring Brandon so you can have their complete attention."

A veil of tears clouded Leah's vision before she closed her eyes for a moment and willed them away. "When they arrive, take them into a conference room and make sure I have enough time to answer their questions."

Kathy laid a hand on Leah's arm. "No one would think less of you if I had one of the attendings tell them."

She straightened her shoulders and assumed a bravado she didn't remotely feel. "It's a part of the job, Kathy." The part she despised the most. "I've had to deal with this type of situation on several occasions. I can handle it."

"Are you sure? Because it's pretty obvious you're about to have a meltdown. Raising a baby and taking on sick kids will wear you out. I know because I raised three of my own after my divorce and worked twelve-hour shifts. You need more sleep."

She also needed less distraction. "You're right. I'm going to have to get more rest." As if that was going to happen with so much weighing on her mind, and the added burden of telling two parents they were about to undertake a long, painful medical journey with their only child.

The nurse patted her back. "As far as Brandon's concerned, you caught it early. If it's ALL, and I bet it is, with treatment he has a good chance of going into permanent remission. But I guess I don't have to tell you that."

Leah sincerely appreciated the nurse's attempts at bringing her around to focus on the positive in spite of the negative news. "You're right, Kathy. He has a solid chance at survival." And that's exactly what she would tell the Myeskys, though the information would still be devastating.

Regardless, Leah had to shake off the melancholy that could hamper her judgment. At least a dozen more patients needed her full attention in the clinic and she had that many rounds to make at the hospital before she could even think about leaving. As it stood now, she'd be lucky to make it home before midnight.

Fortunately, Carly was in good hands.

As soon as he returned to the den from putting Carly to bed, Kevin was met with a chorus of laughter, thanks to his merry band of brothers and one brother-in-law. An hour ago, Aidan, Logan, Kieran, Devin and Whit had shown up in a limo—compliments of Logan's elite transportation company—fresh from celebrating, or lamenting, the end of Kieran's bachelorhood. Since Kevin hadn't been able to attend the party, they'd brought the party to him. But he wasn't exactly in the mood to make merry.

Kevin collapsed onto the sofa and propped his heels on the coffee table. "Mind telling me what's so funny?"

"You are," Logan said. "That pink burp rag makes one helluva fashion statement."

Kevin snatched the towel from his shoulder and tossed it onto the table, producing another round of chuckles. "You're all enjoying this, aren't you?"

"We're just surprised to see how well you've settled in as a father," Aidan added.

Kieran had the temerity to laugh again. "Too bad he doesn't have direct access to the mother."

Kevin didn't care to explain that, but if he didn't, he'd never hear the end of it. "We've agreed to be friends for Carly's sake."

Logan looked stunned. "You mean the two of you are living in this house and you're not—"

"No, we're not, so drop it." Kevin didn't bother to conceal his annoyance.

"You must be off your game," Logan said.

Whit shook his head. "More like out of his freakin' mind. Have you seen her? She's one of the best-looking women he's ever dated."

"She also has a boyfriend," Kieran added.

Considering the phone call Kevin had received a few hours ago, that boyfriend was no longer an issue. Unfortunately, he was now charged with delivering the message to Leah. When and how he would do that remained to be seen.

"You know, I'm the only one who hasn't met her yet," Devin said. "Too bad we don't work in the same hospital. I could've made it a point to check her out just to see if she's as hot as everyone says she is."

"Believe me, she is," Kevin said. Hotter than a Texas grass fire.

When the front door opened, Whit muttered, "Looks like you're about to get your chance to check her out, Dev."

Kevin dropped his feet to the floor and practically vaulted off the sofa, looking a little too eager for someone who wasn't interested in having "direct access" to Leah. The rest of the gang also came to their feet and silently stood at attention.

"Kevin, why is there a limo parked at the curb?" Leah asked as she walked into the room and pulled up short. She then eyed each of the men before turning her attention to the beer bottle on the end table. That's when Kevin realized he was in major trouble.

"Hey," he said. "We were watching the game. Looks like they may go into extra innings."

"Since when does watching baseball require a limo?" She managed a smile, but her tone sounded less than friendly.

"We've been downtown," Aidan said. "Because we knew we'd have a few drinks, Logan loaned us one of his limos."

When Leah shot a glance at Kevin, he raised his hands in defense. "I've been here all night."

"I see," she said, although she sounded like she didn't see anything but a bunch of no-good, carousing O'Briens invading her domain. "Where's the baby?"

Kevin didn't believe her frame could get much stiffer without her body breaking in two. "I gave her a bath and put her to bed a few minutes ago."

Kevin's oldest brother stepped up. "I'm Devin, Leah."

She took his offered hand for a brief shake. "It's good to finally meet you, Dr. O'Brien. I assume you're not on call tonight."

"No, but we were just about to leave." He signaled the other brothers with only a look. "See you later, Kev. And it's nice to meet you too, Leah. By the way, you did a great job in the baby department."

She forced another smile. "Thank you."

The O'Brien boys and Whit filed out of the room, mumbling goodbyes and good-to-see-yous on their way to the door, leaving Kevin alone to face Leah's wrath. As soon as they'd all exited, Kevin turned to Leah and tried on a repentant expression. "I know this doesn't look good, but before you get completely pissed off—"

"I'm supposed to be happy that you're having a kegger when you're in charge of our daughter?" She tossed her keys onto a side table and her lab coat onto the arm of the sofa. "And I thought you'd outgrown that behavior."

His determination to remain composed began to diminish. "I *was* watching her, Leah. And do you see a keg anywhere?"

She walked to the end table and picked up the amber bottle from a coaster. "How many of these did you have?"

"None. I told you I don't drink anymore. But even if I had decided to partake tonight, I would've had only one. Not enough to prevent me from taking care of the baby."

She set the bottle back on the table and faced him, her hands fisted at her side. "Is this the way it's going to be, Kevin? When I call you and tell you I'm going to be late, you round up the guys?"

Resentment began to build over her indictment. "They wanted to stop by and meet their niece, and I wanted her to get to know her uncles. There's not a damn thing wrong with that."

"Except you can't entertain a crowd of men and watch a baseball game and do an adequate parenting job."

He experienced the first bite of true anger. "First of all, they were here less than an hour. Secondly, people have lives, Leah. They visit with friends and family and they still take care of their kids without incident."

"Not if they're drinking."

"I told you, I wasn't drinking. In fact, Logan was the only one with a beer. He brought it with him."

She looked altogether skeptical and equally irate.

"Yes, that's what you've said. But then you've said things before that you didn't mean, haven't you?"

Fury hit him with a vengeance. "Maybe I deserve that for what I did to you." He paused only long enough to draw a breath. "But I damn sure resent the implication that I would do anything to hurt Carly. I'd rather die first."

He spun around and stormed toward the back door before he said something he couldn't take back—again.

When she called, "I'm not finished yet," Kevin ignored the comment and walked onto the deck, slamming the French doors behind him and rattling the glass with the force of his frustration. He sat in the glider, leaned forward and streaked both hands down his face.

He'd known all along that Leah held him in low esteem, and rightfully so. He just hadn't realized how much she hated him. How little she believed in him. After her boyfriend had called tonight, he'd actually fooled himself into thinking there still might be a chance to get back what they once had, only better. At the very least, he might have a chance finally to earn her respect. But a few moments ago, she'd shattered any hope he might have for either. And that tore him up, more than she would ever know.

CHAPTER EIGHT

SHE'D NEVER SEEN Kevin so angry. Nor had she seen him so hurt. Leah should derive some sort of pleasure from the pain she'd clearly caused him, but she didn't. Proof positive that revenge wasn't always so sweet.

After she checked on Carly, Leah went in search of Kevin to offer an apology for blowing the brotherly gathering way out of proportion. She also needed to explain her attitude in an effort to make him understand why she'd reacted so strongly. And that was in all probability too much to expect.

Opting to take the same path Kevin had when he'd rushed out of the den, Leah found him seated on the deck, one arm draped over the back of the cushioned glider, staring at the pool backlit in blue. When she moved in front of him, he didn't acknowledge her presence. Either he was lost in his thoughts, or intentionally ignoring her.

"Just wondering if you had a little salt for the crow I'm about to eat," she said, her attempt at humor falling short.

"Right-hand cabinet next to the stove," he said without looking at her.

"I only wanted to say that I'm sorry, Kevin. I know I overreacted. It's just that—"

"Apology accepted."

Leah didn't believe that for a minute, and she wasn't going anywhere until she felt certain he did forgive her. "Do you mind if I sit down?"

"Suit yourself."

Evidently he wasn't going to be receptive to her at all. No matter. She had a tendency to persist when she wanted something badly enough, and she badly needed him to listen to her. With that in mind, she dropped down on the glider, keeping a reasonable berth between them. "I had a terrible day at work. I know that's no excuse for my behavior, but it did play a role."

At least that got his attention. "What made it worse than any other day?"

As difficult as it would be to rehash Brandon's illness, she felt inclined to explain it all to Kevin. "I had to tell two parents that their little boy is incredibly sick."

"Is he going to be okay?" he asked.

"It's hard to say. He has preliminary signs of leukemia, but he'll have to have a bone-marrow biopsy to confirm which type. If luck is on their side, it's the kind that can be treated with chemo and he could eventually go into permanent remission."

"Chemo is damn tough on adults," he said with noticeable conviction. "I can't imagine how a kid is supposed to endure it."

"With a lot of support from his family."

"How did his parents react to the news?" he asked.

Leah pinched the bridge of her nose between her fingertips when the memory of their faces flashed in her mind. "They took it as well as anyone could, but they were justifiably distraught. At least I could offer them some hope before pediatric oncology takes over. Unfortunately, I didn't handle the news all that well when I first heard it."

"What do you mean?"

"I almost had a breakdown in front of a staff member, and I can't allow that kind of emotional reaction. I have to be compassionate, but I also have to remain somewhat detached."

"You're only human, Leah. And you're way too hard on yourself. You always have been when it comes to your work."

"I don't have a choice, Kevin. I have too much responsibility to let my emotions guide me. I've always been able to keep everything in perspective until today."

"Are you sure about that?"

She had no idea what he was getting at, but she planned to find out. "What exactly are you saying?"

"Sometimes I wonder if every critically ill child that you treat is Carl."

She waited for her astonishment to abate before she said, "I had no idea you remembered that story."

"Even if I hadn't, the fact you named our daughter after him would have reminded me. But I'll never forget the first time you talked about him. I finally realized that night what drove you to be a great pediatrician and an advocate for underprivileged kids. But I also realized that you might have problems accepting the fact that you can't save every child, just as it wasn't within your power to save him."

How well he knew her. Perhaps, at times, even better than she knew herself. "If that's the case, maybe I'm in the wrong profession."

"Maybe the world needs more doctors like you," he said. "You'll just have to learn to accept that you're going to have successes more times than you're going to fail, and that loss is an unavoidable part of life."

"I'll keep that in mind." And she would. "But it's harder now that I'm—"

"Juggling motherhood and medicine and functioning on very little sleep."

Almost exactly what Kathy had told her that afternoon. "Okay, I admit that I'm not getting enough sleep."

"That's why you should let me take care of Carly at night."

Right again, but still… "She's my baby, Kevin. I should be able to strike some balance between my work and caring for her."

"You will as soon as you're through with the training phase. In the meantime, give yourself a break. That's what I'm here for, to lessen some of the burden. I just wish I'd been there from the beginning."

Leah welcomed the cherished memory that floated into her thoughts. A bittersweet memory because Kevin hadn't witnessed the birth of their precious daughter. But at least she could share those moments with him now. "I'm probably biased, but Carly was such a beautiful baby when she was born. She had that gorgeous head of dark hair and the most perfect hands and feet. She was also so tiny, not even five pounds, but thankfully healthy enough to leave the NICU after only a few days."

"Then she didn't have any breathing problems?"

The concern in Kevin's voice led to Leah's reassurance. "They had her on oxygen right after she was born, but she didn't need it for long. She's a fighter."

"She comes by it naturally," he said with a smile. "Did you have a tough labor?"

Leah leaned back against the cushion and returned his smile. "Not at all. I'd barely arrived at the hospital before she was born. In fact, it was so easy, I told J.W. I was all for having at least three or four more." She hesitated a moment before adding, "Under the right circumstances."

He turned strangely sullen again. "*He* was there?"

She could guess where this might be heading. "He wasn't in the room when Carly was born, but he did make it to the hospital about five minutes after I delivered her."

"Did he hold her?"

Here came the paternal jealousy. "Yes, he did."

"That son of a bitch."

Leah flinched over his acid tone. "Look, Kevin, I've known him a long time. It would stand to reason he'd want to be there for me."

"You might want to rethink that after what he told me when he called tonight."

Leah had totally forgotten she'd asked J.W. to call her. From Kevin's reaction, she might not want to know the content of that conversation. Still, she had to ask. "What did he say to you?"

"It wasn't good." He leveled his gaze on her. "Are you sure you want to hear it after the day you've had?"

She worried that J.W. had revealed the particulars of their real relationship. "Just tell me, Kevin."

"He said he'd call back in a couple of weeks, after he returned from a trip with his new girlfriend, Cecily."

Leah was at a loss for words and had no clue how to react. Then something totally ridiculous happened—she laughed for a good minute before she broke down in a rush of tears. Maybe the onslaught of hysterics was in part relief that the ruse had ended. Maybe it was a release of pent-up sadness over Brandon's diagnosis. Maybe she was categorically losing her mind.

"I knew I should've waited to tell you," Kevin said as he stood and walked back into the house. Leah initially thought he'd left her with her misery until he returned a few moments later with a tissue that he handed to her.

She dabbed at her eyes and tried to assume some semblance of calm. "I'm glad you told me. And Cecily isn't a new girlfriend. She and J.W. have been on and off since high school."

Kevin moved back beside her. "Do you want me to beat him up?"

Leah managed another, more subdued laugh.

"Funny, that's what he asked me when I told him about our breakup."

Kevin smiled. "We should just duke it out and get it over with."

"That's not necessary, and I'll be fine. It wouldn't have worked between us anyway." On several counts, the first being J.W. was only a friend, and that's all he would ever be.

"Come here," Kevin said as he wrapped an arm around her shoulder and drew her close to his side. "He didn't deserve you."

Completely sapped of energy, and greatly in need of solace, Leah pocketed the tissue and leaned against him. "Thanks for saying that, and I'm sorry for all the emotional turmoil I've been having lately. It's not only about what happened today. I worry that I'm not doing an adequate job at work. I worry I'm not doing enough for Carly. Did you know I actually forgot she turned four months old yesterday?"

"Day before yesterday," he corrected.

"Now I feel even worse."

He gave her a slight squeeze. "You have a lot on your mind, Leah. You need to relax."

What a joke. "I can't relax. I don't even remember how to relax."

He kissed her forehead. "You're a great mother. And you've always had trouble relaxing for as long as I've known you."

"Not true. I managed to relax with you."

"Yeah, but it took some effort on my part."

It had only taken the even tone of his voice, his touch, his presence. "You've always had this remarkable way of talking me down when I was keyed up."

"I thought you said we never talked."

She'd wanted to believe that their relationship had only been about sex. She'd been wrong. "I guess we did have more than a few memorable conversations."

"Yeah, we did."

Leah had intentionally blocked most of the good times in order to make the ending easier. Not that it had been easy at all. Not that she'd even remotely gotten over his callous phone call. But as Kevin set the glider in motion, and they fell into companionable silence, she secretly acknowledged that she appreciated their renewed closeness, Kevin's shoulder to lean on, his counsel. Not to mention he smelled great, the kind of heady scent that made a woman pleasantly lightheaded. A scent that unearthed recollections of making love while surrounded by fragrant candles, something they'd done a few times at his apartment. Oh, the things they'd done to each other at that apartment…

The play of his fingertips drifting softly up and down her arm was reminiscent of the way he used to touch her. And the longer he continued with his caress, the more she tingled.

She was not a tingler. In fact, she refused to tingle. Okay, Kevin was making her tingle. All over. He had done so many times, and the remembrance of those times, combined with the memories he'd resurrected in the cabana that morning, began to take a toll on Leah.

Right or wrong, she wanted something to erase the re-minders of a horrendous day. Something intimate, like a kiss…or more.

"I can almost hear your thoughts zipping around in that head of yours," he said.

"You have no idea what I'm thinking, Kevin." If he did, he would either jump ship or jump her.

"You're still beating yourself up for not being invin-cible."

She'd moved beyond that, with his help. "Not as much as I was."

"Then you're running through a laundry list of things you have to do tomorrow."

She was composing a mental list of why she should ignore the strong carnal urges that made her want to beg him for a little less talk and a lot more action. "Wrong."

"Then you're thinking that in a couple of hours, just when you've drifted off to sleep, Carly's going to wake up for a bottle."

Now she felt somewhat guilty. "No, but thanks for reminding me."

"Okay, you're mulling over why you're sitting with a guy who blew you off for no apparent reason other than he's commitment-phobic."

A sexy man who happened to be available and familiar. Besides, she didn't want a commitment from him now, just a little comfort.

She lifted her head and looked at him straight-on. "Actually, I was thinking I just wish you would shut up and kiss me."

A moment of indecision crossed his face before he tucked her hair behind one ear and framed her jaw in his palm. He answered her request by brushing his lips across hers, but only briefly. Then he did it again, lingering a little longer this time. On his third pass, he kissed her completely, thoroughly.

How she had missed this, kissing Kevin. She'd missed his gentleness, his incredibly tempting technique. His ability to make her feel so…so…hot. A little moonlight making out was harmless, as long as that's as far as it went. But when the kiss continued, deeper and deeper, Leah longed for more.

As if he'd channeled her thoughts, Kevin slid his hand beneath her top and skimmed his fingertips along her ribcage. Common sense tried to convince her to halt the madness now, but when had she ever been able to lay claim to common sense when it involved him? Before long, she was shifting restlessly against him, silently urging him to go further. To take her to the limit and beyond, as he once had.

When Kevin ran his palm along the curve of her hip and curled it on the inside of her thigh, right above her knee, Leah couldn't stand it any longer. She nudged his hand upward, guiding him to the place where she wanted his attention most.

She left his mouth long enough to whisper, "I need—"

"I know what you need," he said. "Some things you never forget."

When he kissed her again, Leah expected the pull

of the drawstring at her waist, the feel of his fingertips beneath her clothes. Instead, he stroked her through the cotton scrubs, softly at first before applying more pressure. The climax happened so quickly, and with such strength, she shuddered and gasped.

"That didn't take much effort on my part," Kevin said, followed by a low, sexy laugh.

Leah didn't know whether to be mortified or grateful. "It's been a while."

"I can tell." He dropped his arm from around her shoulder. "Now that you're relaxed, it's bedtime."

She wasn't so embarrassed that she wouldn't gladly finish what they'd started, despite the lack of judgment in that. Only convenience sex, as Macy had so gracefully put it. And if she really believed that to be the case, she *was* crazy. "My bed or yours?"

He lifted his arm from around her, pushed off the glider and faced her. "You go to your bed and I'll go to mine."

She felt as if he'd slapped her across the ego. "Thanks, Kevin. You've successfully made me feel like a desperate idiot. If you didn't want to finish this, then why start it?"

"I didn't start it."

Oh, heavens, he was right. "Then why didn't you just tell me you didn't want any part of it?"

He braced one hand on the back of the glider, the other on the arm and leaned forward, so close that she could kiss him again. "If you believe that I don't want to get you naked and get inside you right now, then you don't know me at all."

At least that provided some salve for her self-image. "If that's true, then what's stopping you?"

He straightened and streaked a hand through his hair. "I'm not going to take advantage of you when you're vulnerable. And I won't make love with you unless I'm sure you want to be with me, not because you're looking for revenge or rebound sex."

She should tell him about her real relationship with J.W., but that secret was Leah's last line of defense. A line that had begun to blur. "I don't know what I'm looking for, Kevin." That was the honest-to-goodness truth.

"That's what I thought." Disappointment filtered out in his tone.

She stood and pulled at the hem of her top. "You're right. We should sleep in separate beds and forget this happened." At least she could attempt to forget.

He pointed at her. "And I'm going to take care of Carly tonight so you can get some uninterrupted sleep."

She was too weary to argue with him. "Okay. Anything else?"

When she started forward, Kevin backed up a step. "Yeah. Go to bed before I say to hell with principles and change my mind."

Leah was overcome by an odd sense of power. "Don't worry, Kevin. I'll try to resist the urge to ravish you in the middle of the night. But I make no promises."

She turned and strolled back into the house while mulling over how wrong Kevin had been about her motivation. She didn't desire a diversion. She didn't care for convenience sex. She wanted him—so much she ached. She always had. But having him came with a high price, because she did know Kevin O'Brien.

She knew his innate ability to make a woman feel as if no one else had ever existed. She also knew he had a habit of leaving a trail of broken hearts—hers had been among them. Yet she was tougher now. She could steel herself against emotional entanglement. She could take what he was willing to give as long as she didn't cross the love line.

Of course, she would have to convince Kevin to participate. That would require patience and playing hard to get. Experience had taught her that anticipation was the greatest aphrodisiac on earth.

But was it really worth the risk? Oh, yes, it was. He was.

KEVIN ROLLED OVER in bed, glanced at the clock and realized he'd slept through the night…without getting up once with Carly. He sat up and focused on the monitor's illuminated red light that indicated it was working. Unless the receiver had quit functioning. Or someone had intentionally shut it off.

He suspected who that someone might be. Leah had probably slept in the nursery in order to take the night-shift, ignoring his attempts at giving her a break. At least the arrangement had lasted almost a week. And three days ago, she had finally agreed to let him pick Carly up at noon from day care.

Since then, he'd settled into a good routine with his daughter—he worked in the mornings and played Dad in the afternoons. In the evenings, both he and Leah pretended nothing had happened that night on the deck. But for six solid days, he'd thought about nothing else, while she'd become aloof, plying him with subtle overtures designed to drive him to the brink of madness. An accidental brush against him in the kitchen, walking through the den wearing only a towel and then acting shocked to find him in front of the TV. Sheer torture.

Forcing the thoughts from his brain, Kevin crawled out of bed, put on a pair of workout shorts, and, when he entered the hall, he sought out the person rummaging around in his kitchen. He found Leah standing at the sink, filling the coffee pot with water…dressed in those damnable animal-striped pajamas. Talk about the worst kind of punishment—look but don't touch.

He slid onto a bar stool and folded his hands before him on the counter in an effort to control them. "Where's the baby?"

"Amazingly, still sleeping," she said without looking at him. "I checked a few minutes ago."

"How many times did you get up with her last night?"

She faced him, looking half startled, half confused. "I have no idea what you're talking about. I didn't get up with her once."

Alarms rang out in Kevin's head. "Neither did I."

He raced out of the kitchen and down the hall, Leah following closely behind him. As he grasped the nursery's door handle, one terrible thought whizzed through his mind. She was ill and no one had been there for her. Or she was in her crib, kicking her feet and making unintelligible baby noises.

"Is she okay?" Leah asked from behind him.

Quietly he closed the door and smiled. "She's fine. I'm not sure what she's saying to her hands, but she sounds pretty animated. And since you didn't get up with her, and I didn't get up with her, that means—"

"She slept all night."

Without warning, Leah launched herself into Kevin's arms and wrapped her legs around his waist. He spun her around a few times before sliding her back down to her feet, putting them in close contact with barely any clothes between them. Worse, she didn't immediately let him go. Huge mistake.

A hundred push-ups and a forty-five-minute shower nightly had been the only means he'd had for keeping his libido in check. Bearing in mind his current state, he'd have to resort to two hundred push-ups and spend an hour in the shower before he got on with his day.

With the last of his will intact, Kevin turned his back on her, laced his hands together behind his neck and started toward his bedroom. "Take care of Carly, please. I need a few minutes." He needed a bucket of ice down his shorts.

"Do you have a problem, Kevin?"

He stopped and sent a glance over his shoulder to find her grinning. "You could say that."

"Would it happen to be that exclusively male morning condition known as nocturnal penile tumescence?"

He faced her again at the risk of confirming her diagnosis. "You know how much I love it when you talk dirty to me in medical-speak, but this has nothing to do with the time of day. You just rubbed your half-naked body down my half-naked body. Add that to your ongoing seduction, and that's what's causing my problem."

She looked down at said problem, then back up again. "You had your chance the other night on the deck."

How well he knew that. "We've already been through this, Leah."

"I know, and we need to discuss it further when I come home this evening."

He remembered the e-mail he'd received last night after she'd gone to bed, and the dilemma it presented. "I won't be here when you come home. I have to fly to Atlanta this afternoon."

She frowned. "Why?"

"Because I've been summoned by the magazine's top brass. I tried to get out of it by suggesting a conference call, but they want a face-to-face meeting. It's only a couple of days. I have to play golf on Saturday with the big guns, but I'll be back late Saturday night."

"How convenient. Now you have a real excuse to avoid me."

He rubbed a hand over his jaw. "It's not a damn bit convenient, and I'm not avoiding you."

She crossed her arms beneath her breasts. "Yes, you are. When I come home, you either go to the gym or to the cabana and work out for hours. After dinner, you retire to your office until it's time for the baby to go to bed."

Okay, so he had been avoiding her, with good reason. "I'm just doing what you asked, Leah. Letting you have some quality time alone with Carly."

"You barely look at me, Kevin. I feel like I have some kind of deadly virus and there's no cure."

She did—a viral sex appeal that sent him into a cold sweat. "I'm looking at you now, and it's killing me not to take you back to bed and take care of my problem. But I figured that's exactly what you intended by wearing those damn pajamas."

She shrugged. "I didn't have anything else to wear to bed since I haven't had time to do laundry this week."

Lame excuse, as far as Kevin was concerned. "My housekeeper comes in every Friday morning, which happens to be tomorrow. If you'd let her wash your clothes when she does mine and Carly's, that won't be an issue."

"I'm capable of doing my own laundry, thank you very much."

"Come on, Leah. Admit it. You're trying to keep me hot and bothered."

"I'm not *trying* to do anything, Kevin. Besides, you have a tendency to overheat over fairly insignificant things."

"Like the fact I can practically see through that top you're wearing?" And the effect that his perusal had on her breasts.

She shifted her weight from one foot to the other. "Look who's talking. You're not even wearing a shirt."

He ran a hand down his sternum to the low-riding

waistband on his shorts, only to see how she would react. And she reacted by biting her lower lip. "Does that turn you on? Because now you know exactly how I feel. Or are we engaged in some kind of competition to see who cries uncle first?"

"I believe I did that last week on the deck."

"No, you moaned."

They continued to stand there, facing off, while Kevin envisioned backing her up against the wall and kissing that sly smile off her face. Taking off those man-killing pajamas really slowly…

The sound of Carly's cry temporarily suspended the tension hanging between them, and served as a reminder as to why he couldn't act on his urges. But that tension was going to be present as long as they lived together. And as soon as he could think clearly again, he'd have to decide what to do about it.

"What time do you leave?" Leah asked as she began retreating toward the nursery.

"My flight's at 4:00 p.m." But he had an appointment two hours prior to that. An appointment at the lab, something he wouldn't mention until he had the results, if he even mentioned it then.

When she turned toward the bedroom and gave him a bird's-eye view of her bottom, one of his favorite aspects, Kevin just couldn't help himself. "Nice ass, Cordero."

She opened the door, looking as if she needed a quick getaway. "I'll call the day care and tell them Carly will be there all day."

"And I'll call you tonight."

LEAH HAD WAITED all evening long for Kevin to call. When the phone finally rang, she'd been lounging in the den aimlessly flipping through the channels and thinking about nothing—except him.

She answered with a casual "Hello", and he responded with "Hey."

Now what? Something general would be best. "Did you have a good flight?"

"It was crowded, thanks to the holiday."

Leah hadn't even considered that. "I'd totally forgotten it's July Fourth weekend."

"That reminds me," he said. "I hope you're not on call this weekend because I talked to my mom and volunteered our place for the celebration on Sunday."

Our place. She still didn't view the house as hers. "No, I'm not on call. What do I need to do to get ready for this little get-together?"

"Not a thing. I'm going to grill burgers and the rest of the family will bring something to add to that. They've been doing this so long, they have it down to a science."

They did, maybe, but not Kevin. From what he'd told her in the past, he'd avoided most family gatherings in recent years. "Sounds like it should be a great time."

"And you'll finally get to meet my parents."

Lovely. "I hope they'll be okay with that."

"They'll be fine. Just remember what I've told you about my dad. Prepare for a lot of Irish sayings that make no sense."

She laughed. "I'll remember."

"How's my other girl doing?" he asked.

The way he'd said *other girl* gave Leah pause. "She's been a little fussy, but right now she's sleeping like a baby. Probably because she is a baby." *Real bright, Leah.* "She misses you."

"And I miss her. I miss you, too."

She didn't quite know how to respond to that, so she chose to flip to another subject. "How did your meeting go?"

"Fine. Good actually. They want me to relocate to Atlanta and assume the position of Executive Creative Director. It means a bonus and a salary increase. But it also means longer hours and some travel."

Leah silently scolded herself for caring whether he traveled or not. In the grand scheme of things, it didn't matter. She had her career, and he had his. "Are you going to accept?"

"I'm leaning in that direction. The house is going to be quiet when you and Carly move out. I'll need something to occupy my time. Besides, Atlanta's only six hours from the Jackson area. I could make that drive in a day to see Carly."

"When you're not traveling," Leah added, an unmistakable edge in her tone.

"It's not a done deal yet. I told them I'd give them an answer by September. In the meantime, I'll keep doing what I'm doing from home."

Another topic needed to be broached, and now seemed like a good time for Leah to tackle it. "About this morning, Kevin."

"I know. I kind of lost control of my mouth. I'm sorry."

"No, you're not."

"Okay, I'm not. But I wasn't the only one tossing out the innuendo."

Leah couldn't very well dispute that. "You're right. And while we're being open with each other, I have a confession to make."

"About?"

She drew in a deep breath and let it out slowly. "I fabricated the extent of my relationship with J.W. In reality, he's only a friend."

A span of silence passed before he asked, "Then the two of you weren't a couple?"

"A couple of childhood buddies, but that's it. Granted, he was there for me when Carly was born, but more or less as a surrogate uncle."

"After your reaction when I told you about his girl-friend, I thought—"

"That I was upset over the end of our presumed re-lationship. My crying jag was the result of stress, not J.W.'s girlfriend."

"I'm confused, Leah. Why did you lie about it?"

"I thought that if you thought I was involved with someone else, then what's been happening between us wouldn't happen. And it did work for a while, until J.W. blew it by leaving that message."

"For the record, you don't need protection from me. Like I've said before, I won't do anything you don't want me to do."

And that was the problem. She wanted him to do

anything he'd like—aside from breaking her heart again. "Are you mad?"

"No, I'm not mad. On some level I do understand the self-protection aspect. I'm a master at building walls."

She'd been on the outside of those walls, trying her best to break them down, without success. At least until recently. "You seem much more open than you used to be, Kevin."

"I'm working on it, Leah. But I still have a few issues to deal with."

Continued confirmed bachelorhood could be one of those issues. "Can you elaborate?"

"Let's just say a lot went on in my life while we were apart. Those events caused me to do some serious soul-searching. We'll talk about it when we have more time. It's going to take a while for me to explain."

His cryptic attitude piqued Leah's curiosity. Yet if she pushed him for more information before he was ready, that could lead him to shut down and shut her out. "In the meantime, what do we do about this thing between us?"

"What do you want to do about it?"

Leah hated it when someone answered a question with a question, especially when the answer was risky. "Well, we're both consenting adults. As long as we know where we stand before establishing a physical liaison, that we're going to enjoy each other until I leave, then I see no logical reason why we can't let nature takes its course."

He released a bark of a laugh. "I feel like I just had a session with a relationship counselor."

She always tended to go into analytical mode when

it came to conflict. "In layman's terms, I don't think we're going to be able to prevent what's happening unless one of us consents to being locked in a closet for the next few weeks."

"We both have a free will, Leah. The point is, neither of us *wants* to stop."

How very, very true. "Then we're agreed we're going to quit fighting it?"

"On one condition. I'd like to know that you'll forgive me one day for how I ended it with you."

"I have forgiven you, Kevin. But it's something I may never forget. That's why I have to tread cautiously." Exactly why she had to treat lovemaking with Kevin casually. That could prove to be incredibly difficult, if not impossible.

"Fair enough," he said. "Then we'll let nature take its course."

Leah checked the clock and, after realizing the lateness of the hour, decided the time had come to end their conversation. "Now that we've settled our chemistry issues, it's time for bed."

"Sounds good to me, sweetheart, but since I'm here, and you're there, the bed's not all that appealing."

Little by little, the Kevin she'd known before had begun to surface. The sexy-talking, sweet-nothing-whispering Kevin, who could keep her on a prolonged high with only the sound of his voice. "Believe me, I seriously need to sleep. But I really have enjoyed our talk. It reminds me of the conversations we used to have when you were out of town for an interview."

"Not a chance, unless I say something like this." He lowered his voice and listed a litany of sensual, stimulating and somewhat graphic suggestions about what he'd do to her if he were there.

Leah laid a palm over her rapidly beating heart. "Why, Kevin O'Brien, I'm shocked."

"Are you really? You used to give as good as you got, and if I remember correctly, you didn't utter one anatomically accurate term."

Luckily he couldn't see her blushing. "That was before I was the mother of a daughter."

"It's okay to be bad, Leah. Being a mother shouldn't impact your natural sexuality. Besides, how do you think kids get siblings?"

The smile in his voice brought about her own smile. "Surely you're not suggesting we make a brother or sister for Carly."

A stark, deafening silence ensued, leading Leah to believe his fear of settling down still existed, in spite of his love for Carly. "I'm kidding, Kevin."

"I know you are. Now go to bed and remember what I just said to you a few minutes ago."

"Oh, yeah. I'll go to bed practically on fire with no one to cool me off."

"I wish I could be there to help you out, babe. But if you want me to talk you through it so you can get some relief, I'm game."

"No, Kevin. I just want you to hurry up and come home to me."

CHAPTER NINE

ON SATURDAY EVENING, Kevin came home after 11:00 p.m. to find the den deserted and the house quiet. He was more than a little disappointed that Leah hadn't stayed awake for his arrival, even if he had called and told her earlier not to wait up. Probably just as well. He had an important call to make in private, and if she happened to greet him with a kiss, talking on the phone would be the last thing on his mind.

After entering his office, Kevin closed the door behind him on the chance that Leah might appear. He could have waited until morning, but with his oldest brother's habit of staying up past midnight even when not working the E.R. night shift, odds were Devin was still awake.

When he answered with his usual "Dr. O'Brien," Kevin didn't hesitate to get to the point. "Hey, Dev, I was wondering if you've heard anything on the lab work."

"No, and I didn't expect to hear anything. You dropped off the specimen at two o'clock on a Friday before a holiday. You'll be lucky if you have the results on Monday."

Kevin loosened his tie and shrugged out of his jacket. "Is there anything you can do to rush it?"

"I'll call the lab first thing Monday morning, then I'll call you if I learn anything."

"Thanks. I'm just a little anxious about it." Both anxious and dreading the news at the same time. But he needed to deal with this matter before he laid it all out on the table when he finally told Leah the truth.

"I understand your anxiety," Devin said. "But even if the test shows you're sterile, you still have hope. They've developed a few treatments for post-chemotherapy azoospermia that can result in conception."

"But there's no guarantee."

"Of course not. It's still something positive to go on."

It might not be enough for Leah to permanently figure into Kevin's future. And he wanted her in his future. He'd come to that conclusion over the past two nights when he'd done nothing but think about her. So much was riding on how he handled the revelations about his previous illness, and how she responded. A lot depended on whether she would accept why he hadn't told her sooner, and the possibility that Carly might be the only biological child they could have together.

Right now, he needed to say good-night to her and his baby. "Thanks again, Dev. Guess I'll see you here tomorrow."

"Unfortunately, I'm on call. And I'm expecting the emergency room to be packed with people who've celebrated just a little too much. Ask Leah about it. I'm sure she can tell you a few stories about her E.R. experiences. And speaking of Leah, use a condom, just in case."

He could argue they weren't sleeping together, but he didn't see any reason for that. Not when they were coming so close to taking that step. "Thanks for the info, and I'll talk to you on Monday."

After Kevin hung up, he left his office and on the way to his bedroom, stopped by the nursery first. He opened the door to find the room bathed in muted light from the lamp in the corner, revealing mother and daughter sleeping on the daybed, facing each other, their foreheads almost touching.

Even though a shower and sleep called to him, Kevin couldn't seem to pull himself away from the sight. He leaned a shoulder against the door frame, realizing that moments like these might be few and far between. Or they might never come around again if Leah walked out of his life, taking Carly with her. But as he continued to watch both his girls, he vowed to do everything humanly possible to keep that from happening, unless fate dictated otherwise.

LEAH HAD greatly enjoyed the food, the company, and the simple task of doing nothing except sun-basking. Yet watching Kevin and their baby playing in the pool had been the highlight of her day. Carly wore a pink polka-dot floppy hat that matched her brand-new bikini, exposing a tummy that had filled out in the past few weeks. Kevin had donned a pair of navy swim trunks that gave her a great view of his equally great legs. That and his bare, broad chest provided enough diversion to last almost a lifetime. Almost.

She was astonished at how patient Kevin had been with Carly today, even after coming in late from his trip. So late, he'd said, that he hadn't bothered to wake her. She sincerely wished he had.

While Leah continued to look on, Kevin taught Carly how to splash the water with her tiny fists after relatively few attempts. And from the proud grin on his beautiful face, he looked as if his daughter had accomplished something monumental. She could only imagine how he would react when she took her first steps, when she said her first words, when she rode a bike without the benefit of training wheels. To think that he might not be around to witness those milestones brought about a down-in-the-dumps feeling she couldn't ignore. In a perfect world, they would be the perfect family. Life experience had taught her perfection wasn't always attainable, and that only increased her sense of sadness.

"He looks so natural with Carly."

She managed a slight smile aimed at Mallory, who was seated in a lounge chair next to her. "She's definitely becoming a daddy's girl. He was gone two days and she practically squealed when she saw him this morning." Leah had wanted to do a little squealing, as well, but she'd refrained from appearing to be too excited to see him, even if she was.

"It's going to be hard on both of them when you move back home," Mallory said.

That reality had begun to bother Leah, as well. "He'll be able to see her whenever he's available."

"But it's not the same thing, is it?"

No, it wasn't. Yet Leah didn't see any real choice in the matter. Not unless something drastically changed in their relationship over the next few weeks.

In an effort not to ruin the afternoon completely, she surveyed the backyard and took a quick head count. Whit and Mallory's toddler twins, Maddie and Lucy, had gone into the house with their grandmother and grandfather. Logan and Jenna hadn't come since Jenna was due to deliver any moment; Devin's absence came about because he was playing doctor for the day. That left Corri and Aidan, who were lounging on a blanket beneath a tree with their toddler, Emma, fast asleep beside them. She soon realized one couple was noticeably absent. "Where did Kieran and Erica go?"

Mallory took a drink of iced tea before setting it back in the holder built into the lounger's arm. "When they couldn't seem to keep their hands off each other, my dear husband told them to get a room. And since Stormy is at a sleep-over, I'm assuming they left and did just that."

Not such a bad idea, Leah decided before she pushed those thoughts out of her mind. "They really seem to be crazy about each other."

"They are," Mallory said. After a brief hesitation, she asked, "There's not any chance you and Kevin might become more than just friends again?"

She was surprised that she hadn't heard that question

before now. "We're on different paths, Mallory. I have my career and he has his. We've both moved on."

"Not Kevin. As far as I know, he hasn't had anyone else in his life since the two of you broke up."

Leah suspected Mallory didn't know everything about Kevin's extracurricular activities. Nor did she, and she frankly didn't want to know. "I find it hard to believe that Kevin hasn't been back on the dating scene."

"I'm almost positive it's true. For the most part, he's become a regular homebody."

Leah pondered that for a moment before Dermot O'Brien walked out of the house and took the empty chair beside Mallory. "Are you not going to join your beau and baby in the water, Leah?"

Obviously Kevin's dad was making a huge assumption about her relationship with his son. Yet she felt it would be rude to set him straight. "I'm just enjoying having a day away from work. Between the hospital and the clinic and finishing up the last of my research, I haven't had much time off since I moved..." She certainly wasn't going to be the one to tell Kevin's parents about the living arrangement. "I guess it's been a few weeks."

Whit came up behind Mallory, leaned over and kissed her cheek. "You mean Kevin hasn't given you a break since you moved in here, Leah?"

Mallory pinched him hard on the thigh, causing him to wince and ask, "What did I say?"

Dermot belly-laughed. "Don't worry, daughter. Kieran told me a while ago that Kevin and the lassie were livin' together. Even if I wasn't the wiser, I'm thinkin' that isn't the lad's makeup and girly shampoo in the spare bathroom. And I'm also thinkin' that those items are there to throw this old hound off the scent. Would you and my boy be tryin' to pull the wool over my eyes? Or would you be sharing the same mattress?"

Mallory said, "That's enough, Dad," while Leah internally cringed. Heavens, she should've been a little more discreet with her personal belongings.

"I'm only here until August," she added promptly to clear the air. "I wanted Kevin to have the opportunity to get to know Carly before I return home. That's why I agreed to move in. And in answer to your question, he has his bedroom and I have mine."

Lucy O'Brien picked that moment to exit out the French doors, a plate of golden-brown pastry in her hand. She set the dessert down on the table and regarded Mallory first. "The girls are in the back bedroom taking a nap." She then pivoted toward Leah and asked, "Is that Kevin's loofah in the bathroom, dear, or are you and my son living together?"

Leah's toiletries had served to dig a hole bigger than the Grand Canyon. At the moment, she wished she had a hole to crawl into. "It's not what you think, Mrs. O'Brien. We're friends and nothing more."

"You're the parents of a baby girl." Lucy took a seat across from her husband and shook her head. "I have such a hard time figuring out young people these days. You seem to treat cohabitation as a sport. First Devin and Stacy living together while they were in college.

Kieran and Erica aren't living under the same roof but they might as well be and I know Aidan and Corri moved in together before their wedding and so did Logan and Jenna, even though they pretended otherwise. But the worst scenario…" She shot a quick glance at Mallory then Whit. "All that time the two of you pretending to be roommates while secretly making a baby."

"Making two babies," Whit added with a grin.

Lucy sighed. "The world is changing too fast for me."

"My love," Dermot began. "For what cannot be cured, patience is best."

"And don't cut your throat with your tongue, old man," Lucy tossed back. "You still have to sleep with me."

Dermot winked. "And what a pleasure that is."

Mallory rolled her eyes. "Okay, let's not get into the too-much-information terrain. And let's leave Leah alone. How she and Kevin choose to live their lives isn't any of our business." She put both pinkies in her mouth and blew out a loud whistle. "Bring my niece to me, Kevin."

Whit rested his hands on Mallory's shoulders and faked a frown. "She has baby fever, which means I'm going to be nothing more than a stud to her until we make another one."

When Mallory reached to pinch him again, Whit caught her wrist. "Not this time, lady."

Leah enjoyed the good-natured banter between the family members, but she also experienced a little bout of homesickness. With her parents retired and traveling for the summer, she'd rarely spoken to them lately. Yet when Kevin left the pool carrying Carly, Leah didn't feel quite so lonely. For the moment, he served as a part of her immediate family, if only temporarily.

After wrapping the baby in a towel, Kevin handed her off to Mallory. "She's going to be an Olympian swimmer if I have anything to say about it."

"I thought you wanted a softball player," Leah said.

"No reason why she can't do both."

Leah found herself practically melting over Kevin's grin, and since she couldn't seem to keep her eyes off his bare torso, she thought it best to make a hasty escape, or risk giving herself away. After kissing Carly's cheek, she scooted off the lounger and stood. "I'm going to get something to drink."

"I could use something, too," Kevin said. "I'll be right in."

Without even asking if anyone else wanted anything, Leah rushed into the house, thankful for the cool air drifting over her rather warm body. She attempted to convince herself that her elevated temperature was due to the July sun, even though that sun was starting to set. Like it or not, Kevin had played a major part in her somewhat overheated condition, a condition that had plagued her for days.

Not long after she'd filled her glass with ice, Kevin wandered into the kitchen and slid his shades onto the counter. "When are you going to take off that cover-up, Leah?"

She looked down at the oversized T-shirt that hit her mid-thigh. "When I'm sure everyone's gone."

"Why? I can attest to the fact that your body looks great."

"You haven't seen me naked, Kevin."

"How soon we forget."

"Recently."

"I've come pretty close a couple of times." He walked up behind her and kissed her neck. "You smell like suntan lotion."

She poured tea into the glass, fortunately without spilling it. "You smell like chlorine. You've spent so much time in the water, I'm surprised you haven't turned into a prune."

He clasped her waist and turned her around to face him. "I assure you, nothing on my body is shriveled."

She sidestepped him and moved to the opposite end of the kitchen. "We need to be careful. Your mother and father figured out I'm living here. I wouldn't be surprised if they're developing a few more theories about our relationship as we speak. More accurately, our sleeping arrangements."

He shrugged. "Let them speculate. What we do in the privacy of our home is our business. Speaking of which…" He grabbed a cola from the refrigerator and popped it open. "Mallory wants to take Carly for the night. I told her I'd ask you, but I thought it wouldn't be a problem. She says we should go to dinner or see a movie. Something to get us out of the house. Personally, I can think of plenty to do without leaving the house."

So could Leah. But still… "I don't know, Kevin. A whole night without her? That would be the first time that's happened since I brought her home from the hospital."

Kevin moved so swiftly, Leah didn't know what had hit her until he had her in a luscious lip-lock. Once they parted, he said, "Carly will survive a night without us, and so will you. Besides, I'll keep you occupied."

The thought of being completely alone with Kevin blanketed Leah's arms in goose bumps, belying the warmth that had begun to settle in other unseen places. "We could pick her up around ten."

"Midnight."

"Eleven."

Kevin ran both hands through his damp hair and stared at the ceiling for a moment. "If that's what it takes for you to give us some time alone, then it's a deal. But we're not going to pick her up a minute earlier."

Leah dumped too much sugar into her glass, stirred a good deal of the liquid onto the counter then grabbed a rag and wiped it up with a vengeance. "When is everyone leaving?"

"Soon, I hope."

As much as Leah loved her baby, she felt the same. The sooner everyone departed, the sooner she could relax and not have to watch every word she said around his family. And the sooner she'd be alone with Kevin.

That point-of-no-return moment was almost upon

her. The moment when she'd have to take the proverbial plunge and finally have what she'd fantasized about for days.

And she was absolutely going to jump.

As soon as the last of the family had left, Kevin turned from the door to find Leah had disappeared. He worried she was regretting sending Carly off with her aunt and uncle. Worried even more that she was regretting being alone with him.

After a futile search of the house, he walked back onto the deck to find Leah swimming laps in the pool. He took a seat in one chair and watched her for several minutes until she finally came up for air and started wading toward him.

The automatic pool light had come on, bathing her in aqua blue, making her hazel eyes appear almost translucent. She moved through water like some sea goddess and stepped onto the stairs looking like his favorite fantasy. Although she didn't completely exit the pool, she did finally give him a great view of her body encased in a black bikini. A bikini that wouldn't be considered risqué under any circumstance. The bottoms were cut just below the navel and high on the legs, the top had thin straps and enough of a plunge to reveal some cleavage. He didn't care how tasteful it was, the suit had the impact of a rocket launcher, and he definitely had liftoff.

She rested one hand on the rail and swept the other through the water. "Aren't you going to join me?"

Did monkeys swing from trees? He shifted in the chair and rubbed a palm down his abdomen, drawing her attention. "I don't know. I've been swimming most of the day. Maybe we should talk about this first."

Without advance warning, she reached behind her, dispensed with the top and threw it onto the deck. "Do you still want to talk?"

Oh hell, no. "Is that your version of waving the white flag of surrender?"

"It's black, and I surrendered the minute you walked out here."

Kevin couldn't exactly explain his hesitancy other than he had to be sure she knew what she was getting into. "If I come in there with you, I'm not going to want to stop at just a swim."

"I'm not going to stop you, either."

Leaving all his reservations in the dirt, he had the presence of mind to kick off his flip-flops but didn't even bother removing his T-shirt and trunks…yet. When he stood and started toward the pool, Leah swam away before he even made it down the first step.

Not a problem. He'd worked summers in high school as a lifeguard. Even if that hadn't been the case, he owned enough sexual energy at the moment to shoot him through the water like a human propeller. After only a few strokes, he had Leah in his arms and his mouth covering hers in a kiss that probably *would* be considered risqué under any circumstance.

They treaded water for a while until Kevin moved to the shallow end of the pool, allowing his feet to touch the bottom. Leah broke the kiss first and frowned. "I'm feeling a little self-conscious since I'm almost naked and you're fully dressed."

When she clasped the hem of his shirt, he raised his arms and let her lift it over his head. "Satisfied?" he asked as he watched her hurl it onto the deck.

"Yes, but what did I feel underneath your arm?"

Damn. The scar from the line they'd used to administer the chemo. "I don't know what you mean."

"Lift up your arm and I'll show you what I'm talking about."

He could appease her, or ignore her. "It's probably just the remnants of some football injury."

"I know every inch of your body, Kevin, and I don't remember any scar on the underside of your arm."

"Quit being the doctor, Leah. It's nothing, I promise." He kissed her again. "Now where were we?"

"I believe we were getting you undressed."

As she grabbed the waistband of his trunks, he brought her hands up to his chest. "Don't rush this," he said. "I'm so jacked up right now, it's going to be over before it starts if we're not careful."

She smiled. "Now you know how I felt on the deck the other night."

"I'd like to know how you feel right now." He pressed his palms against her lower back, bent his head and with the tip of his tongue followed the path of a trickle of water sliding down her chest from her throat.

When he closed his mouth over her breast, she arched her back and dug her fingernails into his shoulders. He'd seen her like this before, trembling, needy, hanging on to the last shred of control. And he knew precisely how to deal with this situation.

Kevin pulled Leah's legs around his waist then carried her up the steps and to the blanket Aidan had spread out beneath the oak earlier that day. He set her on her feet and, without saying a word, worked her bathing suit bottoms down her hips. When they dropped to the ground, she stepped out of them and kicked them aside.

He moved back a step and visually traveled down her body, taking in the sight of the familiar territory he'd explored before. But that made the prospect of doing it again no less exciting. "You're as beautiful as I remember."

She lowered her eyes. "I'm ten pounds heavier and I have a few stretch marks and—"

He halted her uncharacteristic self-deprecation with a light kiss. "I said you're beautiful. End of discussion. Besides, you're not in the mood to talk, remember?"

She sucked in a ragged breath. "You're right."

"And I happen to know exactly what you're in the mood for."

Before he could take her down on the blanket to demonstrate how well he knew her, she said, "We can't do this, Kevin."

What a time for her to reconsider. "Whatever you want, Leah. I'm not going to force the issue."

"I meant to say we can't do this here unless you get a condom."

Leah had inadvertently provided the perfect opening. He could tell her they might not need a condom, and why. Or he could just let it go for now, and that's what he planned to do. Maybe he chose not to come clean because the outcome of the test was still unknown. Maybe it was latent selfishness coming into play. Maybe he just couldn't bring himself to confess, not when he could show her how much he still cared for her in the best way he knew how.

Besides, he was, and had always been, much better with actions than with words, at least when it came to personal relationships. Strange considering he made a living with words. But those came easily. Others didn't.

"Kevin?" she asked when he failed to respond. "Are you okay?"

He would be, as soon as he made love to her. "Yeah. I'll be right back."

CHAPTER TEN

VERY EARLY ON in their relationship, Leah had learned one important thing about Kevin O'Brien. He knew what women liked. Countless times he'd taken her into the realm of mindless pleasure with his skill as a lover. But first and foremost, he had a penchant for tempting her straight into oblivion. Apparently that hadn't changed.

While she stretched out on the blanket to await his undivided attention, he stood a few feet away, staring at her until she couldn't stand the suspense any longer.

"Did you suddenly turn shy on me, Kevin, or do you want me to beg you?"

"Once I join you on that blanket, there won't be any turning back."

She only wanted to go forward with no thoughts of the past, or what might have been. Not even what could be. Thinking about any of that would be too painful. "I want to be with you, Kevin. I don't know what else I can do to convince you."

"I'm convinced." He tossed the condom onto the ground beside her and finally slid the trunks down his narrow hips, alleviating any doubts that he wanted her, too. At least physically.

When he moved onto the blanket, he simply took her into his arms and held her for a moment. There was such a surprising tenderness to his kiss in the beginning, but as it had been between them before, passion and chemistry soon took hold.

His lips drifted down her body, and Leah briefly thought about the hazard in allowing this much intimacy. She thought about how easily she could lose herself to him again. But she quickly tossed those concerns aside, closed her eyes and immersed herself in the sensations. A warm breeze blew over her, but it did nothing to lessen the heat. Only Kevin could ease the need, and he did, using his mouth with so much persuasion that she gripped the blanket.

At first he showed some restraint, taking her almost to the brink before letting up without quite letting her down. She knew exactly what he was doing—drawing it out until she couldn't stand it any longer. And just when she'd reached that point, he took her all the way. She couldn't stop the involuntary lift of her hips or the urge to cry out or the climax that came all too quickly. Yet it wasn't enough.

As if he sensed that, Kevin sat up and tore open the foil packet with hands that appeared to be shaking. Leah could relate. She was shaking, as well. As he eased inside her, he let out a long breath and kept his gaze centered on hers. "Stay still a minute," he said. "I want to remember this."

She wasn't sure if he meant he wanted to recall all the times before, or if he was already preparing to say goodbye again. She didn't have time to ponder that when he began to move, slowly, slowly, until he quickened the pace. She became absorbed in the flex of his muscles beneath her palms, the absolute power he held over her. He had always been somewhat of a chameleon during lovemaking—sometimes playful, sometimes seductively taunting—yet he'd never been as intense as he was right now. Especially his eyes that he kept fixed on hers.

Leah sensed a desperation in the way he kissed her, the way he held her as if he couldn't get close enough. The way he spoke to her in a hoarse whisper, describing how she felt surrounding him. How she was driving him *crazy*. He moved his hips against her and touched her in a way that led her to believe he was determined not to find his own release until she found hers again.

She wanted him to stop the pleasurable torment. To never stop. "Kevin, I'm not sure I can take it."

"You can, babe. You will."

And she did, with much more force than she ever thought possible.

Kevin then lost his grip on his coveted control and with one final thrust, he groaned, shuddered and stilled against her.

The sound of their labored breathing cut into the quiet of the night as Leah wondered if her heart rate would ever return to normal. She also questioned if she'd ever be able to find another man who could make love to her as well as Kevin could. If she would always compare any other man to him. If any man would ever measure up.

After a time, Kevin rolled to his back, taking her with him. For several moments, they stayed that way, holding each other, her head resting on his chest and his fingertips drifting up and down her back.

When the lure of sleep began to settle over her, Leah realized the time had come to face reality. "We need to pick up our daughter."

He brushed a wayward lock of hair away from her cheek and tucked it behind her ear. "Mallory plans to keep Carly until morning unless we call and say we're on our way. I don't want to make that call."

She lifted her head to look at him. "I don't know, Kevin. She'll—"

"—be fine. I'm sure she's already asleep and I don't see any benefit in dragging her out of bed in the middle of the night. I'm also not ready to end this. We have to make up for lost time."

That did make sense, at least the part about not disturbing the baby. But Leah still had a few misgivings. Making up for lost time could carry a high cost.

He kissed her again. Leisurely, seductively. "Be with me, Leah. In my bed, all night. You won't regret it."

She wasn't so sure about that. Yet spending the next few hours in his bed, making love with him again, making more memories, overrode the last of her concerns. "Okay, I'll stay with you." At least for the night.

WHEN THE cell phone rang not long after dawn, Kevin issued a mild curse as Leah moved to the opposite side of the bed to answer it. Even though he was sapped of strength after his and Leah's recent lengthy shower, he wouldn't mind another round of lovemaking before they both had to face the day. Those plans could go awry if she was being summoned to work, which he suspected to be the case.

"Hi, Mom."

So much for the work theory. Kevin glanced at Leah who pulled the sheet up to her neck and sent him a forlorn look.

After a long pause, Leah said, "Really, everything's great. Carly's great. I'm great."

Kevin rested his forearm over his eyes and tried not to listen to the conversation. But he couldn't help wondering exactly what her mother had said when Leah responded with, "No, I haven't done anything stupid."

He assumed that probably involved him, and he hoped Leah believed her own words. After she had all day to think about what they'd done last night—and this morning—she might question her intelligence.

A few minutes later, Leah hung up the phone and collapsed back onto the pillow. "That was my mother."

"I'd already figured that one out." Kevin rolled to his side to face her. "Kind of early for her to be calling."

"Yes, but she knows my schedule. She also wanted to let me know that she and my dad are leaving for Europe this evening. And more importantly, she learned that a local pediatrician is retiring in two months. He's looking for someone to take over his practice."

Kevin was overcome with a strong sense of urgency and fear that he was on the verge of losing her if he didn't act fast. Needing her closer, he patted the empty space beside him. "Come here. You're too far away."

She scooted over and settled in the crook of his arm. "I have to get ready for work."

"It's still early," he said. "And I'll pick Carly up from Mallory's and keep her with me all day, if that's okay with you."

"It's more than okay, Kevin. You've proven you can take care of her, so I don't see why she needs to go back to the day care while we're here."

He liked that he'd earned her trust when it came to Carly, but he didn't care for the *while we're here* part. "What time do you have to be at the hospital?"

"Not until eight-thirty."

Kevin glanced at the clock. "It's a little past seven."

She tapped her fingertip against her chin. "Now I wonder how we can spend the next hour or so. Wait, an idea is coming to me."

Leah streamed her hand down his belly, but before she reached her intended target, Kevin clasped her wrist and halted her progress. "As much as I appreciate your idea, we need to have a conversation first." The content of that conversation was still up for grabs.

She lifted the sheet and grinned. "Looks like one of your brains likes my idea better."

Yeah, that brain definitely had a mind of its own. "I want to talk about last night."

She shifted away from him and focused on the ceiling. "You don't have to say anything, Kevin. I know what last night meant. We both needed the diversion."

"Diversion?" That sent Kevin off the bed to retrieve a pair of pajama bottoms. Once he had those on, he perched on the edge of the mattress beside her. "It was a hell of a lot more than that to me, Leah."

She closed her eyes and said, "Don't complicate matters by saying what you believe I want to hear, Kevin."

"Don't tell you that I don't want you to leave at all?" He had absolutely no right to ask that of her, but he hadn't been able to stop the words from spilling out of his mouth.

Her eyes snapped open and she pinned him in place with a serious stare. "You don't mean that."

"Yeah, I do." And he did, even though the request was ill-timed.

"You're only offering because of Carly," she said.

He understood why she would think that. "I'll admit that I can't stand the thought of you taking her away from me. But I don't want to lose you again, either."

She sat up and hugged her knees to her chest. "Let's just say I'm crazy enough to consider taking our relationship to the next level. Where do we go from here? You're planning on relocating to Atlanta and I'm going back to Mississippi. And even if we worked that out, do we just live together?"

He wanted more than that, but he couldn't offer

more right then. Not until he knew for certain what the future might hold. "I don't have all the answers yet, but living together is a start. I don't want to give up on us."

"And what happens if you get tired of me?"

"I'm not going to get tired of you, Leah. I…" Damn, he wasn't any good at voicing emotions. He never had been. "I care about you."

"I care about my car, too, Kevin. And if I recall correctly, last summer in Cabo you said you cared about me and then you broke it off a week later."

"It's different this time."

"What's different, Kevin, other than we have a child together?"

He had to tell her the truth, but he couldn't tell her everything until he acquired all the information. Information that hinged on the results of the lab work that he'd begun to dread with every passing moment.

But he could tell her the one thing that might make a difference, something he'd never told her before. He decided to reserve that declaration for later, when it might be his last hope. "Like I've previously stated, I had my reasons for doing what I did last year."

"You're right. You've already said that. But at some point in time, you're going to have to share those reasons with me."

"I know, but it's going to take more time than we have this morning. When you get home tonight, I promise I'll tell you everything then." In the meantime, he intended to take advantage of the hour they had left, and continue to hope.

He rolled to his side, tugged her back into his arms and kissed her. But before he could utilize his powers of persuasion, the phone rang again. This time, his phone.

If Mallory didn't still have temporary custody of his daughter, Kevin wouldn't have bothered to answer. But because of that, he fumbled for the phone and barked out an irritable. "Yeah."

"Are you going to be home this afternoon?"

He sat up and draped his legs over the side of the bed. "It's barely morning, Devin. I'm not even awake." Not necessarily the case. His brother's question had him wide awake.

"I thought I'd stop by around three."

"Any particular reason?" Kevin suspected he already knew the reason.

"I had to come into the hospital early and I did what you asked. I put a rush on your results. But I'd rather not discuss it over the phone."

Kevin didn't want to discuss it at all, particularly if Devin felt as if he needed to deliver the news in person. That could mean only one thing. "Sure. I'll see you then."

He hung up the phone and fell back onto the bed, feeling as if his entire world was on the verge of coming apart at the seams.

Leah curled up close to his side and kissed his neck. "Is everything okay?"

Not in the least. "Yeah. Devin's going to be in the neighborhood and he wanted to stop by to see Carly."

Only one more lie to add to the many he'd been doling out.

She lifted her head and surveyed his face. "Are you sure nothing's wrong?"

Kevin wasn't sure about anything, except that right now, he only wanted to lose himself in Leah, before he had to face reality once more.

With that in mind, he brought her back into his arms and whispered, "Now let's get back to your idea, while we still have time."

THE SOMBER LOOK on his brother's face as he stood on the porch served to confirm Kevin's suspicions—the news wasn't going to be good.

As badly as he hated to hear the truth, he opened the door anyway, stepped aside and said, "Come in, Dev."

They walked the hall in silence and when they reached the den, Devin slipped his hands in his pockets and looked around. "Is Leah here?"

"Not yet."

"The baby?"

"Taking a nap. And now that we've established who's home and who isn't, just say what you need to say."

Devin withdrew an envelope from his inside jacket pocket and handed it to him. "This is everything in writing."

Kevin withdrew the piece of paper and scanned the text, some of which made little sense. "Care to interpret?"

"The good news is, you're still producing sperm.

The bad news is, you're producing so few that you're clinically sterile."

No matter how much he'd prepared to hear that word, Kevin still wanted to hit something. "This is pretty damned ironic. A couple of years ago, being sterile might not have been that big of a deal. But now that I have Carly, I feel like nothing about my life meant anything before her." Before Leah, too. "But I guess this is fitting punishment for all my previous sins."

Devin shook his head. "You won't ever get me to buy into the whole divine retribution thing, Kevin. Too many bad things happen to good people and that includes you, too. You didn't warrant getting sick any more than anyone else."

He'd never heard that coming from his oldest brother before. Not once had he ever expected he would. "I've done some pretty sorry things, Dev."

"What? You broke a few hearts and had a tendency to be self-absorbed? That doesn't make you bad to the bone."

The women who owned the hearts he'd broken would probably argue with that assertion. "You forgot about what I did to Corri."

"And Aidan thanks you every day for getting out of her life so he could step in. Maybe your methods of ending it were suspect, but they've both forgiven you for that."

Almost the same method he'd used to break up with Leah, only he'd graduated from a written note to a brief phone call. "When I tell Leah the truth about every-thing, she's not going to forgive me."

Devin looked incredulous. "You mean she still doesn't know you were sick?"

"No, and I'm still not sure I should tell her." He held up the lab slip he'd been gripping in his fist. "Not after seeing this."

"Like I told you, Kevin, this isn't the end of the world or your future fatherhood. You could still have biological children if you undergo one of the current treatments. The pregnancy would have to be assisted, meaning insemination or in vitro, but having another baby isn't impossible."

Truth was, he didn't want any more babies unless he could have them with Leah. "It doesn't matter. Even if Leah does accept that we might not have any more kids, once she finds out I've lied about everything, she'll never want to come near me again."

Devin contemplated him a few moments before he asked, "Do you love her, Kevin?"

"Yeah, I do." He laid the paper down on the coffee table and looked at his brother straight-on. "But I'm still going to lose her, Dev."

"You might, but you'll never know for sure unless you tell her everything. And if you don't do that, then you'll definitely lose her because she's going to leave if you don't at least try to convince her to stay."

Kevin felt Leah's inevitable goodbye as keenly as he'd felt his daughter's joy when she smiled and her distress when she cried. He also sensed the formation of the impenetrable emotional armor that he'd used for self-protection most of his life.

Leah had been the only living soul able to breach that armor, and he realized she would probably try again. In the next few hours, he would have to decide if he'd let her.

THE MOMENT she'd arrived home, Leah felt as if the events of that morning had never happened. After all his talk of a future together, Kevin hadn't seemed at all pleased to see her. In fact, he'd barely spoken to her. He'd been totally withdrawn during dinner, answering her questions about his day with the baby in short, terse sentences. Then he'd mumbled something about working on his column before retiring to his office. She hadn't seen him since.

Perhaps he'd had too much time to think about his proposal and suddenly remembered he didn't want to settle down. Regardless of his reasoning, she intended to break the silence and find out what was going on.

As soon as she put the baby to bed, Leah went straight to Kevin's inner sanctum, geared up for a confrontation. She expected to find him seated behind his desk typing away, not stretched out on the small black leather sofa, staring off into space.

She crossed the room and hovered above him. "Writer's block?"

When he turned his head toward her, she was taken aback by the dejection in his red-rimmed eyes. "I haven't been writing. I've been thinking."

"About?"

"Us." He sat up and leaned back against the cushions. "We need to talk."

"That's what you said this morning."

"After this conversation, you're probably going to want to disregard everything else I said this morning."

"I don't understand." Oh, but she feared she did. All too well.

He moved to the edge of the sofa, draped his arms over his knees and lowered his head. "You should keep your plans to move home next month."

She released a mirthless laugh even though she wanted to scream. "Wow, Kevin. And they say women are fickle. This morning you wanted me to live with you indefinitely, and now you want me to go. But I'm not surprised, which is why I didn't get my hopes up." Not true. She *had* begun to hope. To imagine a life that included him.

He still refused to look at her. "I've changed my mind because I can't give you what you need."

History was repeating itself. "I know, Kevin. You can't commit to one person. You can't love only one woman, if you're even capable of loving anyone at all."

Finally, he raised his eyes to her. "You're wrong, Leah. I love you. I was in love with you when I let you go last summer. I've never felt that way about anyone before you, or since."

Once the shock subsided, Leah struggled to find her voice. "If that's true, then what do you think I need that you can't give me?"

"It doesn't matter."

Leah's anger, sadness and frustration melded together, creating the perfect emotional storm. "It does matter to me, damn it. You owe me an explanation, Kevin, and I'm not leaving until you give me one."

He rubbed both hands over his face before turning his gaze on her. "You're right. But you're going to need to sit down."

She backed up and dropped into the chair across from him. "Okay. I'm ready." But was she really?

"Before I left for Atlanta, I had some lab work done," he began. "I found out the results today."

This could be worse than Leah had imagined. "Oh my God, Kevin, are you sick?"

"I'm sterile."

The pronouncement took a moment to sink into Leah's jumbled mind. When it finally did, she said, "Evidence to the contrary is asleep in the nursery." Surely he wasn't suggesting… "If you're intimating she's not your child—"

"I know she's mine, Leah. This resulted from something that occurred after we broke up." He paused a moment before adding, "Actually, it's the reason why I broke it off with you."

"None of this makes any sense, Kevin." And she needed for it to make sense.

He clasped his hands tightly together. "Right before we went on the trip to Cabo, I went in for a physical. You might remember that I had a lot less energy than usual."

"You thought it was all the traveling you were doing at the time."

"It wasn't. I'd contracted idiopathic aplastic anemia. I spent six months undergoing transfusions and when that didn't work, Kieran agreed to donate his bone marrow. He saved my life."

That explained the renewed relationship between the brothers. "And he was the perfect genetic match because he's your twin."

He streaked a hand through his hair. "Lucky for me. But the chemotherapy caused—"

"The sterility." At least now some things were falling into place for Leah. "The scar underneath your arm is from the PICC line they used to administer the chemo."

"Yeah."

Myriad questions ran through Leah's mind, but the most important took precedence. "Why didn't you tell me when you were diagnosed?"

He lowered his eyes again. "Because you had enough to worry about with your work."

"Not a good enough reason."

"I thought I might die, and I didn't want to put you through that."

Now they were getting somewhere. "I'm a doctor, Kevin. I could have helped you through the process, answered all your questions. I could have been there for you."

The look he gave her was so full of sorrow and remorse, it stole her breath. "I didn't want you to see me that way."

She wanted to cry for him and everything he'd endured. She wanted to shout at him for letting pride stand between them, even though she did understand that on some level. She wanted to turn back the clock and start over. But that was impossible.

He rested his arm over the back of the sofa and turned his profile to her. "You have every right to be furious with me."

"When I consider all the opportunities you've had to tell me, yes, that makes me extremely angry," she said. "But when I think about how we could have been there for each other during your illness and my pregnancy, it makes me sad that we've wasted so much time."

A stretch of silence passed before Leah posed another all-important query, one that could determine if he had— or hadn't—changed, depending on the answer. "If you could do it all over again, would you have told me?"

"I honestly don't know, Leah. Maybe if I'd known about the baby, but then maybe not. It was my burden to bear, not yours."

Not the answer she'd been seeking, but at least now she knew what had to be done, even though the decision made her heartsick. "You're right, Kevin," she said as she stood. "You can't give me what I need, and it has nothing to do with future children. My parents fostered almost one hundred kids during a thirty-year span and there are plenty more out there who need homes and families."

His gaze zipped to hers. "If I'd known for certain you felt that way, I would've asked you to marry me this morning."

This morning, she might have said yes. "That's just it, Kevin. You didn't ask me how I would feel about anything. You didn't give me any choices. You're so used to pushing everyone away that you don't know anything else. Commitment means sticking it out through good times and bad, that old for-better-and-worse aspect. I have no way of knowing if you're going to leave when the going gets tough, or at the very least close me out. That ability to share has sustained my parents and your parents throughout their marriages. I won't settle for less."

"I don't know what you want me to do, Leah." His voice was even and emotionless.

She wanted him to seem less resigned. She wanted him to argue his case, lower his guard. To fight. "If I have to tell you, Kevin, then there isn't any hope for us at all."

She could be judging him too harshly, closing her mind to the possibilities, but she didn't want to risk being hurt by him again. Better to end it before that happened, despite the pain she was suffering right now. For him and for her.

"What do we do now, Leah?"

"I don't know, Kevin." And she didn't. "I do know I'm not sure if I can live here with you."

"Just don't do anything rash," he said. "I need to have Carly in my life until you leave next month. I won't pressure you for anything more. I won't even touch you. I might not like it, but I'll do what I have to do as long as you'll stay."

"I'll have to think about it."

And that's what she would do, probably the rest of the night. That, and have a good cry.

CHAPTER ELEVEN

BECAUSE OF Carly's nonstop crying, Kevin almost didn't hear the bell. "Thanks for coming, Mom," he said after he opened the door and led Lucy into the kitchen.

"Thank you for calling me, dear." She set her purse and keys down on the counter and practically beamed. "I'm glad to help. Now let me have that little one."

Kevin handed the baby over to her grandmother and leaned back against the cabinet to watch them interact. Fortunately Carly's fascination with her grandmother's string of pearls had halted her tears. If he'd known a necklace would stop her crying, he would've contacted the local jeweler and ordered one ASAP.

"She's been irritable all morning, and she doesn't seem to want to eat," he said even though Carly looked anything but upset.

Lucy didn't seem to mind that the baby grasped the pearls and stuck them in her mouth. "She could be teething."

"Isn't it kind of early for teeth?" Each day brought more milestones, and Kevin didn't like that she was growing so fast.

Lucy patted Carly's bottom as she strolled around the kitchen. "Your brother Aidan had his first tooth at four months and a full mouth by ten months. I had to wean him earlier than the rest of you."

When his mom moved back beside him, Kevin pushed a lock of hair away from Carly's forehead. "She just doesn't seem normal today. I'm probably over-reacting, but it's tough when I can't make her happy no matter what I do."

Lucy inclined her head and surveyed him a few moments. "Now you understand, don't you?"

"Understand what?"

"How it feels to love someone more than yourself."

In a way, that hurt. But she was absolutely right. "Yeah, I do. And I'm assuming this worrying thing isn't going to stop any time soon."

"It never stops, Kevin. That's why I was so cautious when it came to you. I had a difficult time getting over almost losing you when you were born. And I know how much you've resented it, both when you were growing up and more recently, during your illness. Any time a child suffers, so does the parent if they're any kind of parent at all."

Finally, an admission of guilt from his mother. But somehow Kevin didn't feel as if he needed to air his grievances any longer. She'd done what she'd done out of love for him. "It's okay, Mom. Being a father has helped me comprehend your tendency to watch me like a hawk and worry incessantly. I'm over it."

"Then you forgive me for choking you on a regular basis with the apron strings?"

He grinned, but it quickly faded. Smiling wasn't something he felt like doing after his confrontation with Leah. "Yeah, I forgive you. As long as you forgive me for all the times I've screwed up. Apparently I didn't learn from my mistakes because I've done it again."

She laid her palm on his cheek. "What have you done, sweet boy?"

He took Carly from her and placed her in her swing, then pulled out a chair at the breakfast table. "Sit down. This might take a while."

After she complied, Kevin recounted what had transpired between him and Leah three days ago. He ended with, "I've done permanent damage to our relationship by not telling her what she needed to hear. Now there's no hope for us."

"Oh, Kevin. There's always hope. You only have to keep believing, and take advantage of the time you still have with her."

Carly let out another sharp cry, causing Kevin to pull her out of the swing's seat. "This is what I mean, Mom. She sounds like she's in pain."

Lucy frowned and felt Carly's forehead. "She doesn't seem to have a fever, but that doesn't mean anything. I've heard a terrible stomach flu is going around. She could have picked that up from the day care."

"True. But so far she doesn't have any other symptoms."

"If she has a virus, you'll know soon enough. And if that happens, be sure to give her clear liquids. Little ones dehydrate very fast." She glanced at her watch and pushed back from the table. "I'm sorry to have to run, but I have a library board meeting in fifteen minutes. I'll be glad to come back afterward if you'd like."

Kevin came to his feet with Carly wrapped securely in his arms. At the moment, his daughter didn't seem at all distressed. Maybe she *was* teething. "I appreciate your advice, Mom." But he still wasn't clear on a plan of action when it came to his problems with his child's mother. "I wish I knew what to do."

"That's easy, dear. Call Leah if you're still worried about the baby. After all, she's the pediatrician."

"I meant I don't know what to do about Leah. The thought of her leaving is killing me."

Again she patted his cheek. "If I were you, I'd start by giving her some space."

"SHE'S FINE, Kevin."

Considering the way Carly looked at the moment, content to watch her mobile in the crib, kicking her feet against the mattress like a battering ram, Kevin would have to agree. "You didn't hear her this morning, Leah. Her cry was different, like something was hurting her."

She moved back from the crib and faced him. "I checked her temp and felt her belly. Since she doesn't have any other symptoms, she probably just has a little tummy ache. The cereal might not be agreeing with her."

"She refused to eat any cereal," he said. "She took part of one bottle this morning and she hasn't wanted anything else since. In fact, she hasn't eaten all that well for the past few days."

Leah checked her watch. "It's only a little past noon. Try giving her another bottle in an hour or so."

"And if she doesn't want it?"

"Then call me and we'll go from there." Leah leaned over and kissed Carly's cheek. "Mommy's going back to work now. Try to be good for Daddy."

When Leah left the room, Kevin followed her into the hall. "Do you mind stopping for one second to talk to me?"

She turned and folded her arms beneath her breasts. "Is that what this is about Kevin? You called me home so we could talk?"

He decided to try and lighten the mood, kill her with kindness and turn on the charm. "You're the best pediatrician I know."

Leah's cynical expression said she wasn't impressed. "I'm the *only* pediatrician you know. However, Carly has her own doctor and you'll find her number taped to the side of the refrigerator. But I'm fairly sure you knew that, which brings me back to my first theory. Asking me to come home wasn't only about Carly."

Out went the charm and in came the ire. "If you sincerely think I'd use our daughter as a pawn, then your opinion of me is worse than I thought."

She rubbed her temples and studied the floor. "I don't know what to think. I do know that Carly seems perfectly okay, and that we could have handled this over the phone."

Even a deep breath did nothing to calm his anger. "That would suit you just fine, wouldn't it? No personal connection whatsoever. You haven't spoken to me in three days and you won't even look at me now."

She finally raised her gaze to his. "You promised me you wouldn't do this."

"I promised that I wouldn't touch you. That doesn't mean we can't be civil. Maybe that's what's wrong with our daughter. She senses the tension between us and she's not any happier about it than I am."

"Maybe it's just the heat, Kevin."

Houston might have been suffering from a severe heat wave for the past two weeks, but the temperature in the house had been ice-cold. Kevin would have pre-ferred a nonstop rant to Leah's silence. "Maybe you're bent on punishing me for the next few weeks."

She looked away again, indicating to Kevin that he'd touched on the truth. "I really need to go," she said. "We're holding a wellness clinic at the hospital this af-ternoon and I have to examine at least twenty kids. I also need to talk with Macy before I begin my appointments."

Dread bubbled up inside him. "What about?"

"As I said the other night, I don't feel comfortable living here with you. I believe it would be best if I take Carly and move back to the apartment."

Panic replaced the dread. "Don't do it, Leah. Don't take her from me yet. Just let me have this time with her."

"I have to go back to work, Kevin."

"Go ahead." He made a sweeping gesture toward the den. "Go back to work. But first, I want to set the record straight. You can hate me for as long as you'd like and you can take Carly out of the house or out-of-state, but I'm not going away. I plan to be in my daughter's life permanently, and that means birthdays and graduation and, God willing, walking her down the aisle. If I had a choice, we would share all of that together as a family. But since that's no longer an option, you still need to think long and hard about how you want to deal with our future relationship. Any conflict between us is going to affect Carly."

"I can't do this now, Kevin." She started down the hall, but before she disappeared around the corner, she faced him and said, "If you notice any more symptoms with the baby and you're concerned, bring her to the hospital and ask for Dr. Roundtree. She's the head of pediatrics. She'll page me."

He wanted to prevent her from leaving, to plead his case one more time, to convince her that he had, in fact, become the kind of man who could be faithful and steady and honest. He wanted to tell her once more that he loved her. Instead, he let her walk away, knowing it was only a matter of time before she walked out for good— unless he could find a way to convince her that they belonged together. If only he had a clue how to do that.

Tʜᴇ ᴄᴀꜰᴇᴛᴇʀɪᴀ was crowded with both staff members and patient families, yet it didn't take long for Leah to spot her former roommate seated near the window. Not many surgical residents looked like blonde-bombshell debutantes. "Do you have a minute?" she asked as she reached the table.

Macy looked up from the sandwich she'd been devouring and waved a hand toward a chair. "Sit. You look like hell."

Leah felt like hell. She took a seat, scooted the chair up to the table and clasped her hands in a death grip before her. "I need to ask a favor."

"As long as it doesn't involve babysitting. You know how I suck at that."

"I want to move back in with Carly, if that's okay."

Macy seemed genuinely taken aback. "What happened with you and the jerk?"

Leah released a dejected sigh. "It's a long story."

"Did he do something vile? Because if that's the case…" She came to attention, picked up a butter knife and held it up like a scalpel. "Just tell me where to find him."

"It's complicated, Macy. Things happened that I didn't plan." Making love to him again. Falling in love with him again, as if she'd ever really fallen out of love with him. "Now everything seems to be spinning out of control and I need to take myself out of the situation."

Macy tossed the knife aside and leaned back in the chair. "You've been sleeping with him."

"Only once." And they hadn't done much sleeping. "Actually, four times. In about twelve hours."

Macy's eyes went wide. "Four times? I didn't know the guy had it in him. I didn't know you had it in you."

"Needless to say, it's been a while." For both of them.

"And now you've let all those fuzzy feelings enter into the mix." Macy looked mildly disgusted. "Did I not warn you about this?"

All the warnings in the world couldn't have prevented Leah's feelings for Kevin from resurfacing. Even now she still loved him, something she didn't dare admit. "It's not just about the sex, Macy. A few days ago, I learned exactly why he broke it off with me."

"Another woman?"

"Aplastic anemia."

Macy tapped her chin. "That's a new one. I've heard 'a dog ate my cell phone' and 'I'm moving to Malaysia to live in a hut,' but I've never had a guy invent a disease as an excuse."

Her former roommate had always been the skeptic when it came to relationships. Leah had begun to conclude that maybe Macy was justified in her skepticism. "He didn't invent the illness. He underwent a bone-marrow transplant about eight months ago."

"Obviously he came through it okay."

"Yes. Only, with the chemotherapy, he might not be able to have—"

"Any more kiddies. No wonder he wanted to claim Carly."

"Having more children wouldn't have mattered that

much to me. At least not to the degree Kevin assumed it would. But that was only one reason he kept the truth from me."

"What are the others?" Macy asked.

"He didn't want to put me through the rigors of his illness and disrupt my career."

Macy smirked. "I can't believe I'm going to say this, but my opinion of the lothario just elevated. Who would've thought the guy had some honor? But I'm not getting why you want to move out now that he's come clean."

She was surprised to hear Macy say anything favorable about Kevin, and that she was suggesting Leah stay in the relationship. "The problem is, he didn't tell me the minute I moved in with him. He's also had many opportunities to let me in on the secret since then."

"But wouldn't the point also be that he did finally tell you?" Macy asked.

Here came the complicated part. "Yes, but he also said that if he could do it over, he still wouldn't tell me because it was his problem, not mine. And that's the whole crux of the matter. He has no idea what committing to someone really means. As far as I'm concerned, I can't stay involved with anyone who's not going to be open and forthright and willing to share in whatever life throws at you."

Macy sat silent for a while, looking thoughtful. "Does it ever get tiresome, being so rigid that you can't bend even a little and accept that people make bad mistakes for good reasons?"

Surely she hadn't heard her friend correctly. "I don't know what you're saying."

Macy sat up straight and folded her arms, looking every bit like a disapproving parent morphing into lecture mode. "Let's just think about this a minute. He didn't tell you in the beginning that he was sick to protect you. You told him you had a boyfriend, a blatant lie, to protect yourself. And if I recall, you didn't try that hard to get in touch with him when you found out about the pregnancy, which also leads me to believe that had to do with self-protection. Am I on the right track?"

Leah hated to admit Macy had made some valid points, so she wouldn't. "Regardless, I can't live with him any longer. It's too painful knowing that we might not settle our differences."

"You'll never settle them if you take off now. Unless your dilemma involves his refusal to make a real commitment, not whether he's able."

"He wants to marry me. I just don't feel like I can trust him to stick around if things don't go well."

Macy took Leah's hands into hers. "You know I love you like my favorite laparoscope, Leah. You are one of the best and brightest docs around. You're going to be a rock-star pediatrician. But right now you're acting so damn stupid because you can't see what's right in front of your face."

Had Macy really called her stupid? "Would you care to explain my apparent lack of intelligence?"

Macy held up her pointer finger. "First of all, unless

Kevin's turned out to be a crappy father, it's not a good idea for you to uproot Carly and deny her the opportunity to bond with him." She joined her middle finger with the first. "Secondly, you might stop and consider why you're really running away."

Clearly Macy was bent on dissecting Leah's motives. "I didn't realize you've changed specialties from surgery to psychiatry."

"I'm just shooting straight, Cordero, like I always do. From what I gather, you're afraid of losing Kevin because you've seen so much loss in your lifetime. Both with the kids that your parents fostered when you were growing up and the kids you doctor now. You're shutting out the possibilities because it's easier to protect yourself from facing that loss again. But as they say, 'Nothing risked, nothing gained,' and all that jazz."

Though Macy could very well be correct on all counts, Leah felt that her heart couldn't take another loss if it involved Kevin eventually walking out on her again. But she would agree that her friend's statement about Carly's relationship with Kevin happened to be on target. "You're right about one thing. I shouldn't move the baby now, particularly since we'll be leaving for Mississippi in a few weeks. She should get to know her dad better in the time we have left in Houston."

"Then you don't see any kind of future with the other babe?" Macy asked.

"Not at this point in time. Not unless Kevin finds a way to prove to me that he is in the relationship for the long term."

"Then maybe you should give him a chance to do that." Macy pushed back from the table and stood. "I'm off to surgery, but I'm glad we had this little talk, Dr. Cordero. Good luck with your quandary, but remember, given time, these things have a way of working themselves out. I'd bet my Harley that something will happen to move you off high-center. And when it does, you may find me and tell me I'm right about everything."

WHEN CARLY began to cry, Kevin returned to the nursery and lifted her from the crib. "Hey, kiddo. I know exactly how you feel."

He retrieved a bottle from the kitchen and carried his daughter into the den where he kicked back in the lounger and tried again to feed her. And again she refused, her cries increasing in volume. He gave up the battle with the bottle and held her against his shoulder until her sobs turned into sniffles. At least he'd discovered how to quiet her for the time being. After a few minutes, he sensed she'd fallen asleep and he thought about putting her back in the crib so he could get to work. He had a few résumés for prospective reporters to go over for the magazine. He had some baseball stats to analyze. He needed to come up with a topic for his next column.

But as he continued to hold his daughter, Kevin realized he didn't have anywhere else he wanted to be. Although he intended to stay in her life, as he'd told Leah earlier, he wouldn't have many opportunities like this after August. Maybe even after a day or two if Leah cut bait and ran back to her roommate.

Kevin closed his eyes and decided a little nap couldn't hurt in light of his lack of rest over the past few nights. He didn't know when he'd drifted off, or how long he'd been asleep, but he did recognize his daughter's distress when Carly tensed in his arms, drew her legs up and released an ear-piercing wail like nothing he'd ever heard before.

He cradled her in his arms and noticed the ashen color of her skin, the way her chest rose and fell rapidly, as if she struggled to breathe.

As fear for his child took hold, Mallory's words filtered into Kevin's mind.

...don't let anyone fool you into thinking that men don't have instincts when it comes to their children. All you have to do is listen to those instincts...

His instincts screamed that his baby girl was in serious trouble.

"YOU'RE NEEDED in the E.R. stat, Dr. Cordero."

Leah removed the stethoscope from her ears and regarded the lanky second-year resident standing in the exam-room doorway. "I'm not covering the E.R., Paul."

He stepped into the room and grabbed the chart from the counter. "I know, but this has to do with your daughter. I'm here to take over for you."

Either Kevin had panicked, or something was seriously wrong with Carly. Leah had a terrible feeling the latter was true.

After muttering an "Excuse me" to the mother of the

preschooler she'd been examining, Leah rushed out of the room and sprinted to the bank of elevators that would carry her down to the emergency room. She punched the down button several times and when the car didn't immediately arrive, she opted to take the stairs two at a time. She arrived on the first floor and pushed past several patients as she headed straight for the staff entrance, pounding out the code twice before the doors finally opened.

Once inside the corridor containing the nurses' station, Leah bore down on the unit clerk seated behind the counter. "My daughter is Carly Cordero-O'Brien. Where is she?"

"In six," the young woman said, followed by, "Your husband's in there with her now, Dr. Cordero."

Because Carly's well-being was first and foremost on her mind, Leah saw no reason to correct the woman's conception of her and Kevin's marital status. Instead, she rushed down the hall and turned the corner to find Alice Roundtree standing outside one cubicle with Kevin. Sheer dread slowed her steps, sent her heart rate on a marathon.

When Alice caught sight of her, she waved her over. "Here she is now."

"Where's Carly?" Leah said when she reached the pair.

"The team's working on her now, so you need to remain here for a few minutes."

The bitter taste of bile rose in Leah's throat. "Working on her?"

"It's intussusception, Leah," Alice said.

The word wasn't foreign to Leah, only entirely un-expected and frightening. "I just left her not more than a couple of hours ago, Alice. I can't believe I would miss that diagnosis."

Normally Alice's kindly smile would be comfort-ing, but at the moment it looked strained. "You've learned through your training that it's sometimes easy to miss," she said. "First of all, it's more common in male infants than female, and secondly, it's deceptive in its presentation. Not to mention you were thinking like a mother, not a doctor. As physicians, we some-times go into denial when it comes to our own children's health because we find it unimaginable that our babies would get sick."

"That's no excuse, Alice."

"You're only human, Leah. If it makes you feel any better, when my son was three, he fell off a playground slide and cracked his clavicle." She aimed her smile on Kevin. "That's his collarbone. I wrongly assumed that since he was trying to climb the bookshelves that evening, he was fine. I didn't have it x-rayed until the next day, and that was only after he said 'ouch' when I tried to dress him that morning."

That provided Leah with very little consolation. "When Kevin called me home to check on her, I palpated her belly and I didn't feel a thing. She seemed perfectly normal at the time."

"Again, that's the nature of this disease," Alice said.

"Could someone please explain to me what's going

on with my daughter?" Kevin asked, stress apparent in his face and tone.

"I was just about to go into that before you arrived, Leah," Alice said. "Unless you'd like to do it."

Every medical term Leah had stored in her brain, every piece of knowledge she'd gained in a ten-year span, temporarily disappeared. "Right now I can't think, so you go ahead."

"There's a section of Carly's intestine that has folded over itself like a telescope," Alice continued. "Normally it takes a non-invasive procedure to put it back into place, but I'm afraid so far that hasn't worked. We're going to have to take her to surgery."

Surgery. The word went off like a detonated bomb in Leah's head. "You've tried everything?"

Alice rested a gentle hand on her arm. "As much as we're willing to try. She's showing signs of acidosis, and she's a little shocky, so we need to act quickly."

The world suddenly seemed surreal, rendering Leah speechless. When she swayed slightly, Kevin put one arm around her shoulder as if he sensed her knees might buckle. "Then you believe this is absolutely necessary," he asked as if he was ready to assume control. Leah was ready to let him.

"In my medical opinion, this is the best option for Carly," Alice said. "And if Leah were treating someone else's child, she would agree."

The same nurse Leah had spoken to earlier approached them, clipboard in hand. "Here's the consent forms for the baby's surgery, Dr. Roundtree."

When Alice offered the documents to her, Leah froze. Kevin immediately took the clipboard, flipped through the pages and scribbled his name, as if he sensed the urgency of the situation.

After reality forced its way into Leah's hazy mind, she finally snapped to. "I want to scrub in for the procedure."

"That's not warranted or advisable," Alice said. "Franklin's waiting in the O.R. and he's the best pediatric surgeon in the state." Again she turned to Kevin. "One of the perks for being affiliated with this hospital."

Leah didn't care if the Surgeon General had agreed to do it, she still wanted to be present. "She's my child, Alice. She needs me—"

"To be her mother, not her doctor."

Leah turned at the sound of the familiar voice coming from behind her. A voice belonging to none other than her former roommate. "How did you know she was here, Macy?"

"I saw her name on the surgery board," Macy said. "And I'm going to scrub in, not you."

"But you don't do pediatrics."

"You are absolutely correct. Usually I avoid it like bridal gowns. But since this is a very special rug rat who requires very special attention, I'm making an exception. You may kiss my ring later." She topped off the comment with her trademark grin.

Admittedly Leah felt somewhat better knowing that Macy—who rightfully carried the reputation of one of the most talented senior surgical residents—would be there to look after Carly. Yet she wouldn't feel at all settled until this ordeal was over and she was assured her baby was fine. "I need to see her before they take her in."

Alice opened the door and peered into the room. "They're bringing her out now. But we only have a few minutes."

When they rolled the gurney through the open doorway, Leah took her place on one side while Kevin moved around to the opposite side. Even after all the times she'd dealt with sick children, nothing compared with viewing the nasogastric tube and IV invading her daughter's tiny body. Nothing hurt more than knowing she couldn't make it all better this time.

"Hey, sweetie, Mommy's right here," Leah said as she touched Carly's hand, fighting tears that she refused to let fall until later. A war she almost lost when Kevin leaned over the railing, kissed Carly's cheek and murmured, "Daddy's here too, baby girl. And I'll be here when you wake up."

While she was on the verge of falling apart, Kevin seemed so confident, so strong. Yet she recognized that he, too, was as torn up over their daughter's illness when she noticed the turmoil calling out from his eyes.

Before they wheeled Carly away, Leah kissed her forehead and smoothed a hand over her hair. When her baby began to cry, she started to ask if she could ride up in the elevator with her, but she wasn't certain how much longer she could hold it together. Instead, she watched as Macy accompanied her child on the first part of a journey in which Leah couldn't take part.

"How long will the surgery last?" Kevin asked Alice once the elevator doors closed.

"At least an hour. Until then, all you can do is wait."

CHAPTER TWELVE

IT HAD to be the longest hour of Kevin's life. And still, fifteen minutes after that time frame, no word from anyone that the surgery had finally ended. At least now he fully understood what his mother had told him—having a child did mean loving someone more than yourself. If he could take Carly's place, he'd gladly do it. Anything to stop his baby's suffering and Leah's too, although she seemed to prefer suffering in silence.

Since they'd moved from the surgery waiting area to the staff lounge, at Leah's insistence, they'd barely spoken to each other. He'd chosen the sofa in hopes that she would join him. Instead, she sat alone in a chair across from him, her bent elbow braced on the arm, her palm supporting her jaw. Her expression seemed relatively blank and that worried Kevin more than if she were shedding uncontrollable tears. Maybe the shock had yet to subside, or maybe her silence meant something else altogether.

"Are you not speaking to me because you think this is somehow my fault?" he asked.

"It's no one's fault."

At least she wasn't blaming him or herself. "Then why won't you talk to me?"

"Because I don't feel like talking." She afforded him a cursory glance. "You really shouldn't be here, Kevin."

She couldn't be serious. "If you think I'm going to leave Carly when she's going through this just because you don't want me here—"

"I meant you shouldn't be at a hospital. Undergoing chemo compromises your immune system."

"My immune system is fine. I've been released by my doctor and I don't have another appointment scheduled for six months."

"That's good." She sounded polite and noncommittal, but at least she seemed concerned about his wellbeing. He was more concerned about his daughter's health.

Kevin checked the clock on the wall and noted another five minutes had passed since the last time he'd looked. "Why do you think it's taking so long?"

"Surgery doesn't follow an exact timetable," she said as she kept her gaze leveled on the door, her tone still flat.

Kevin lowered his head and swiped a hand over the back of his neck. "I screwed up more times than I can count. I hurt people I loved and I had moments of pure worthlessness. For those reasons, maybe I got what I had coming to me when I was sick. But Carly hasn't done anything to deserve this, and that's why this is so damn wrong."

"I know, but as I've told you before, I see it every

day, children suffering for no apparent reason with horrible outcomes."

That sent another round of questions into Kevin's mind. Questions he feared asking, yet he had to know the answers. "I need you to tell me every possible scenario, Leah. Anything that could happen, no matter how bad it might be."

"You don't want to know, Kevin."

That's when he realized the extent of the burden she bore from the weight of her medical knowledge. "Yes, I do want to know. Everything. I can handle it."

When she fell silent again, Kevin thought he might have to force the issue, until she finally said, "If the laparoscopic procedure doesn't work, they'll have to open her up. There's also a possibility a portion of her intestine might have to be removed if it's necrotic. She could have a reoccurrence in the next few days, although that's not common unless there's another underlying condition."

"Is that likely?"

"Not usually, but anything's possible."

He sensed she was still holding back. "What are you not telling me, Leah?"

"She could die."

The declaration had the impact of a gut punch. "That's not going to happen, Leah. It *can't* happen."

The door opened, followed by, "We came as soon as we got your message."

Kevin turned his attention from Leah to his mother, who rushed in, sat beside him and embraced him tightly. His father entered the room at a much more leisurely pace and remained standing, looking as if he wasn't sure what to do next. He glanced at Kevin then at Leah and asked, "How is our little lassie?"

"She was stable when they took her into surgery," she said, sounding every bit the doctor. "As far as we know, the procedure is still going on."

Lucy rested her open palm below her throat. "I feel horrible that I didn't insist Kevin bring her into the hospital immediately when I saw her this morning."

When Leah leveled her gaze on him, Kevin regretted not telling her about his mother's visit or that he'd called his parents a little while ago. "I asked Mom to stop by the house when I first started noticing Carly's change in behavior," he explained. "I wanted to make sure I wasn't jumping to the wrong conclusion."

"And I thought she was probably teething, Leah," his mother added. "Had I known it was this serious—"

"It's okay, Mrs. O'Brien." Leah sent her a small smile. "I missed the diagnosis and I'm a doctor."

"This surgery will correct the problem?" Dermot asked.

"It should." Leah came to her feet and retrieved a cup of coffee from the carafe set out on the counter. She then turned and said, "Would anyone else like a cup?"

"I wouldn't mind one," his mother said as she rose and joined Leah.

Dermot took the spot his wife had just vacated. "The waiting is the worst part," he said. "I remember when Kevin was born and they whisked him away before we had officially welcomed him into the world. My wife did not leave the hospital until they turned this laddie loose."

"I had three little boys under the age of six at home," Lucy added. "For almost a month, Dermot had to take care of them and a newborn by himself."

That was the first time Kevin had heard that part of the story. "You didn't go home with Kieran?"

Lucy shook her head. "I couldn't leave you all alone in that place."

Kevin almost couldn't get past his incredulity. "But didn't Kieran need you, too?"

"Yes, but you needed me more." She came back to the sofa and perched on the arm. "Just like Carly needs both of you now and even after she's grown with a family of her own." She gave Kevin a meaningful look. "Of course, in some ways she'll always need you. It reminds me of that Chinese proverb—'To understand your parents' love you must raise children yourself.'"

When Leah abruptly turned toward the counter, Kevin suspected she might be crying. His dad seemed to have noticed, as well, as he stood and said, "My love, let us go buy that little bear you were eyein' when we passed the gift shop."

Lucy looked at him as if he'd lost his faculties. "I'd like to be here when the surgery's over, Dermot."

His dad nodded toward Leah, who still kept her back to them. "Kevin will give us a shout on the cell phone if we're not back by then."

After glancing at Leah, awareness dawned in Lucy's

expression and she came to her feet. "That's a wonderful idea, dear."

Kevin stood and gave his dad a brief hug, grateful for his astute observation and the opportunity to be alone with Leah. To console her, if she'd let him. "I'll definitely give you a call as soon as we know something."

The minute his parents were out the door, Kevin walked up behind Leah and rested a hand on her shoulder. "Are you okay, babe?"

When she turned to speak, Kevin witnessed the protective wall she'd erected begin to crumble when a few tears slid down her cheeks. Tears that she quickly wiped away with her fingertips. When he tried to hold her, she put up her hands to ward him off and said, "Don't."

Regardless of how badly that stung, he refused to give up. "You told me you didn't know if you could trust me to hang around if the going got tough," he said. "I'm here, Leah. For you and for Carly. Let me help you get through this."

She strode to the window, again keeping her back to him. "I can't afford to need you."

And again he moved behind her and rested his palms on her shoulders. "But you do need me, and I need you. I love you, Leah, more than you'll ever know."

"Don't do this to me, Kevin."

He turned her around to face him. "Just because you don't want to hear it doesn't make it any less true."

When Leah's bravado completely shattered, Kevin pulled her into his arms and was thankful that this time she didn't resist. Instead, she clutched the front of his shirt and pressed her face against his chest, her whole body shaking from her sorrow. For several moments, he held on to Leah, telling her everything would be okay, anchoring her, as well as himself.

When the door opened, Kevin glanced over his shoulder to see Macy enter the room. "Sorry to interrupt," she began. "But I'm here to give an official report if the two of you are done cuddling."

Leah pushed away from Kevin, looking like some teenager who'd just gotten caught necking with her boyfriend in a back seat. "Is it over?" she asked as she grabbed a tissue from a holder set out on the counter.

Macy untied the surgical mask hanging around her neck and tossed it into a nearby trash bin. "Yep, and it was pretty amazing. Franklin took that little kink in Carly's belly and slid it right back into place, and he did it through a scope. She's good to go, or she will be in a few days."

"Thank God," Leah murmured.

Kevin's sentiments exactly. "When can we see her?"

"Right now, but you'll only be allowed to stay for a couple of minutes, and that's only because Leah has clout. Otherwise, they'd make you wait until they moved her out of recovery."

When Macy and Leah exited side by side, Kevin trailed behind and listened while they exchanged information about technical details that meant nothing to him. A conversation involving sats and output and anesthesia that was beyond his comprehension. On the one hand, he felt like an outsider looking in. On the other, for the first time he truly saw Leah as a doctor, a concept that had been almost abstract until now.

They pushed through a set of double doors, rounded a corner and entered an area housing rows of beds cordoned off with curtains. Unwanted memories of his own experience rushed back into Kevin's mind. He hated hospitals. Hated the sterile scents and the drone of monitors, the somber atmosphere. But those things he hated also symbolized life-sustaining treatment. This time, his daughter's life, he realized when Macy led them to a cubicle in the corner where Carly lay on a white-sheeted bed, a miniature yellow robe dotted with red teddy bears covering her torso, her eyes closed against the fluorescent lights.

She had so many tubes snaking out from various parts of her body that Kevin didn't know where some began and others ended. Leah moved to the side of the bed while he hung back, almost afraid to come any closer, as if he might break her if he so much as breathed on her.

Leah pressed her knuckles against Carly's cheek. "Her color looks good."

As far as Kevin was concerned, his daughter looked completely defenseless, and he felt totally helpless.

"She's a little trooper," Macy added. "Right now I have a diseased gallbladder with my name on it, so I need to go. And so do you. You two can see her again when they move her to the pediatric ICU in about an hour."

Kevin's stomach clenched. "Why the ICU?"

"It's standard," Leah said. "If all goes well tonight, they'll move her to a room in the morning."

Macy turned to Kevin and pointed at him. "You, take care of both of them, unless you'd like to audition for lead soprano in a choir."

He didn't particularly care for Macy's threats, not when he intended to take care of his daughter and Leah at any cost. But he wasn't sure how well he could do that until he had some time to regroup.

On that thought, he pressed a kiss on Carly's forehead and backed away from the bed. "See you soon, sweetheart."

He led the way out of the recovery room at a fast clip with Leah following not far behind. They retraced the path they'd taken earlier but this time Kevin opted to bypass the lounge, seeking some form of refuge where he could think.

"Kevin, where are you going?" Leah called out as he kept traveling down the hall. He raised a hand in acknowledgment but he didn't speak. Right now, he couldn't.

After finding an exit, Kevin shoved through the glass door and located a small alcove at the side of the building, away from humanity where he could sort through his feelings alone. He leaned forward against the brick wall and rested his forehead on his bent arm.

The fear for his daughter's well-being was so acute, he found it hard to breathe.

Boys don't cry.

The words echoed in his mind, reminders of a time when he'd been a kid too small in stature to manage his own battles without his twin's assistance. But he would pick fights anyway. He'd learned to kick hard and wound with words. He'd learned how to toughen up, to shield his emotions long after he'd grown enough to hold his own. Those habits had followed him well into adulthood, influencing every relationship he'd ever had, until he'd eventually discovered that using charm as his weapon of choice worked well. It was nothing more than a means to hide the scrawny kid who in some ways still existed. The kid who would rather fight than admit he was outmatched.

He was tired of fighting but he worried that if he did finally cry, he might never stop. The tears fell regardless of his concerns, silent and unseen. Kevin let the emotional dam shatter completely, in turn releasing years of bottled feelings. A final act that signified his transformation was complete. Almost complete, because he still couldn't imagine revealing his grief to anyone, not even Leah. Especially not Leah.

And although he did feel somewhat better, an all-too-familiar loneliness prevailed. Maybe that was the last phase of his redemption—learning that nothing hurt worse than experiencing your anguish alone.

"HERE'S DADDY, Carly." Leah turned the baby around in her lap so she could face the hospital-room door where Kevin now stood. His hair was shower-damp, his jaw not quite clean-shaven, his T-shirt and jeans faded but not at all unpleasant. Nothing about him was the least bit unpleasant, Leah realized as he walked to the rocker and took their daughter into his strong, solid arms.

After Carly grabbed his bottom lip, Kevin pulled her hand away and kissed her palm. "Did you and your mom have a good afternoon?"

"We had about an hour together alone, Kevin. I thought you were going to stay home and get some sleep." For the past five days, he'd kept vigil over their daughter almost 24/7 and the stress had begun to show in his dark eyes.

When Kevin sat on the sofa, Carly immediately rested her head on his shoulder and stuck two fingers in her mouth. Leah found that remarkable since she'd been squirming and fussing for the past half hour. Clearly now that her daddy was back, all was right with her world, and that gave Leah pause. If she moved back to Mississippi—correction, *when* she moved—Carly was going to miss him terribly. Then again, so would she.

"You must really be behind on your work," she said, clearing all thoughts of August from her mind.

He nodded at the black case sitting on the nightstand. "I've been working on my laptop when she goes to sleep. I also convinced a unit clerk to log me on to the hospital's wireless network, but don't tell anyone. I don't want her to get into trouble."

Leah couldn't help but wonder exactly what he'd done to convince her. "Did you promise her a little slap and tickle in the supply closet?"

He frowned. "I said please."

She felt somewhat shamed over sounding like a snippy, jealous lover. Frankly, she *was* jealous. She'd seen the way women looked at him, from the lab techs to the ladies who delivered the meals. Every time she noticed one of those stealthy glances, she'd wanted to shout, "He's mine, hands off." Yet she had no good reason or right to do that.

When Kevin rubbed his eyes with his free hand, she said, "You look totally worn out. I'll stay in the room with Carly tonight."

"Since she's going home in the morning, I'll stay. I can tolerate this sorry excuse for a hide-a-bed one more night. You go home and sleep."

Stubborn, sexy man. "You need the sleep more since you haven't let me stay in here even one night."

"No, you've stayed in the on-call room and made a trip in here every fifteen minutes. You're the one who needs the rest because I'm not dealing with patients all day."

"Maybe we should toss a coin," she said.

"Maybe we should can the arguing and both stay. I'll take the chair."

She rolled her eyes. "That's ridiculous. You're going home to sleep in a decent bed and I'm staying. That's final."

He grinned. "Not if I beat you to the sofa first, and I'm already here."

Obviously he wasn't going to bend in this instance. "Fine. I'll sleep in the chair."

"Neither of you will be sleeping in the chair or on that sofa," came from the vicinity of the door, specifically from Kevin's mother, Lucy, who walked in with her jubilant, hulking husband.

Dermot stopped in the middle of the room and saluted, his grin almost as wide as his belly. "O'Brien parents, reportin' for duty."

Lucy approached Kevin and held out her arms. "Let me have this precious little one."

Kevin stood, handed the baby to his mother and patted his dad's back. "I didn't expect to see the two of you again today."

"We never left," Lucy said. "Jenna's in labor in the maternity ward."

Dermot checked his watch. "She should be poppin' out another O'Brien within the hour."

"Then why aren't you there?" Kevin asked.

Leah was wondering the same thing. "I'm sure they would love for you to be present when the baby's born."

Dermot looked as if he'd eaten something sour. "I am a firm believer in keeping watch in a waiting room, lass."

Lucy strolled around the room when Carly began to fuss. "He faints at the sight of a blister. Besides, Logan knows we're here with you, and he'll let us know when we have our new grandson. In the meantime, Dermot and I decided that the two of you need a break. That's why we're going to take a shift and watch Carly so you two can spend the night at home."

"What do you mean a shift?" Kevin's tone reflected the same confusion Leah was feeling.

Dermot put both pinkies in his mouth and whistled, earning a scowl from Lucy and a trembling lip from Carly. On cue, the O'Brien siblings filed in—Devin in scrubs and lab coat, Aidan in suit and tie, Kieran in T-shirt and workout pants and, bringing up the rear, Mallory wearing business casual. They lined the wall as if they were ready to pass inspection.

"I've invited the clan here to help out with the baby tonight, and they will each do their part." Dermot faced the children and assumed the role of master drill sergeant. "Children, your ma and me will stay until nine since my bones are too old to be sleepin' on a sofa. Who will be next?"

"I will," Devin said. "I'm manning the E.R., but not until midnight. But I need someone to take my place fifteen minutes before that since I have to drive to my hospital."

Mallory raised her hand. "I'll come back then, but I promised Whit I wouldn't be home much later than 2:00 a.m., like he'll really be up then."

Aidan chuckled. "Oh, he'll be up, all right, since you're baby-making."

"Watch your mouth, young man," Lucy scolded.

Kieran took a step forward. "I'll be here at two. I'll stay as long as I need to since I'm not sleeping much these days."

"Pre-wedding jitters?" Kevin asked.

"Erica's withholding sexual favors until the wedding," Aidan said, earning a sneer from Kieran and a stern look from his mother. "If you can stay on until six, Kieran, I'll stay until nine. Corri should be through throwing up by then."

Mallory leaned forward and stared at Aidan. "Pregnant again?"

"Yeah."

A round of mild congratulations followed, and Leah found it remarkable that the family treated pregnancy as an everyday occurrence. Obviously it was for them.

"Then I believe we're set," Lucy said. "We'll be back in the morning so the two of you can sleep in a little later."

"Do we have any say in the matter?" Kevin asked. After they all responded with "No," in perfect unison, he sent Leah an apologetic look. "Are you okay with this?"

How could she protest such a kind gesture? She couldn't, even if it meant being alone with Kevin for the first time in a week. That concept made her both foolishly excited and extremely wary. "It's fine, as long as it's not going to be too much trouble for everyone."

Dermot slid his hands in his pockets and rocked on his heels. "No trouble a'tall. But first, I have a story to tell you, Leah." When all five offspring groaned simultaneously, he held up one hand and silenced them. "Kevin's ma landed in my county in Ireland many a year ago, and when I set eyes on her, I knew I could never be without her again. That is why I traveled across the ocean to this great country, leaving my ma and da behind, to make her my bride. I can only imagine how sorry my life would be without her."

"Is there a point to this, Dad?" Kevin asked, his voice laced with impatience.

"Yes, son. The point is, get your head out of your arse and don't let this lass get away." That prompted a few chuckles from the onlookers before he continued with his directive. "You take her home, talk to her and once you're done foosterin'—"

"Leah, I know that sounds dirty," Lucy interjected, "but it means wasting time."

"As I was sayin'," Dermot continued. "If you haven't convinced her to be your bonnie bride with talk, then do the rest of your talkin' in bed."

Lucy scowled at him. "You could have gone all day without saying that, old man."

Aidan laughed. "Looks like you're going to sleep on the sofa anyway, Dad."

Dermot wrapped his arm around Lucy's shoulder. "My love, when we've had our spats in the past, the makin' up between the sheets was the best part, even if each time we made one of these ruffians."

She sent him an affectionate smile. "If that were true, Dermot, then we would have at least six hundred children, not six."

"Too much information, Mom," Mallory muttered. "May we be dismissed now before we're subjected to any more disturbing commentary on yours and Dad's love life?"

"Not so fast." Logan rushed into the room, camera

in hand and a proud look on his face. "I want you all to see Patrick Avery O'Brien. Eight pounds, five ounces, and the best-looking kid in the universe."

Everyone gathered round to see the newest O'Brien on the digital screen, except for Leah and Kevin. She was still reeling from the shock of the stories and the offer, and the hint of regret in Kevin's eyes indicated what was holding him back. When he took the baby from his mother and held Carly close, he confirmed Leah's conjecture. He needed to have his own child in his arms to remind him of what he already had, not what might never be. She sensed he was hurting more than he would ever let on, and that was still a problem. If only he would let her in, then maybe there could be a chance for them. But following Carly's surgery, he'd established his determination to deal with his feelings on his own when he'd left the hospital without any explanation.

Realizing she'd forgotten her manners, Leah crossed the room and held out her open palm. "Can I take a look?"

Logan grinned and handed her the camera. "My pleasure."

Leah studied the digital image of the sweet, dark-haired, round-cheeked baby boy who looked none too happy about being thrust from the safety of his mother's womb into a brightly lit and foreign world. "He's beautiful, Logan," she said as she returned the camera to him. "Tell Jenna congratulations."

"He looks a little like our former mailman, Mr. Finklestein," Kieran said.

Logan gave his brother a look that could wither a wash pot. "Just wait until you have your first, Kieran. If he inherits your ego, his head will be twice as big as his body."

Lucy flapped both hands and shooed them all toward the door. "Go and leave us all in peace, but be back on time. Logan, we'll be down to see the baby before we go."

Following their goodbyes, the kids quickly exited, exchanging barbs and banter on their way out.

Lucy made her way back to Kevin and held her arms out. "Now it's time for the two of you to run along so I can give our granddaughter her bottle and put her to bed."

But before she could retrieve Carly, Dermot took the baby into his beefy arms and turned her around. "You both must remember, this wee one is a gift. She brought the two of you back together twice now, first with her birth and then through a wretched sickness that should teach you both how fast life can turn like a spindle right before our eyes. She will suffer more if the two of you cannot grant each other grace and honor her with your love for each other."

Lucy slipped her arm around Dermot's waist. "Your father's right, Kevin. She deserves that much."

Dermot handed Carly back to Lucy, his expression still somber. "Leah, although he was a bit of a hellcat when he was a boy, Kevin has grown into a good man. And though he's a slow starter, he loves you, lass. If you have any feelings for him, then it would be my greatest wish that you tell him so that he will stop mopin' like a wolfhound." Dermot then pointed at Kevin. "You must eat your pride like it is an All Saints' Day feast, boyo. And do not come back in the morn and tell me you've settled nothing."

ONCE THEY ARRIVED at the house, Kevin wasn't sure where to begin, but an apology for the coercion by committee seemed like a good place to start. "Sorry for the familial ambush."

Leah toed out of her shoes, dropped onto the den's sofa and crossed her legs on the cushions. "It's okay. I found your parents' story interesting. I don't remember you telling me about how they met."

Kevin took a chance and opted to sit beside her, keeping a decent space between them. "I've never thought much about it." Until this evening, when the message hit home. "But I can relate to what my dad was saying."

She grabbed a throw pillow and hugged it tightly. "How so?"

"I felt the same way about you the first time I saw you. I just didn't realize it until recently. And that's why I'd be willing to forget Atlanta and move to Mississippi if you just say the word."

Her expression showed her surprise. "But what about your family, Kevin?"

"You and Carly are my family, Leah. And I love you both more than any job offer."

"I love you, too, but I wonder if that's enough. We still have other issues to deal with."

"It's a start." Time to address those other issues. "The other day, after I saw Carly in recovery, I couldn't get out of that place fast enough. That's why I went outside and cried like a baby. I can't even remember the last time I did that."

She rested her palm on his arm that he'd draped over the back of the sofa. "Oh, Kevin, that's what I'm referring to. You should have let me be there for you like you've been there for me during this ordeal."

"I know, Leah. I'd never felt so alone as I felt in those moments. I never knew how much I needed you until then."

She went back to the pillow and began twisting the corner. "Macy mentioned something to me the other day, and I realize she's right. I've been so afraid of losing you again that I've set up a self-fulfilling prophecy. If I continued to believe you're going to leave me eventually, then I would never have to face that loss. So I'm not exactly blameless in this situation, either."

He took her hand and when she didn't wrench it out of his grasp, Kevin considered that a small victory. "I promise you this. I'm going to spend every hour of every day until you're through with your fellowship proving to you that I'm serious about not giving up on us. And if that doesn't convince you, I'll be in Mississippi every weekend, maybe even during the week, until you know for sure that I'm in this for the long haul."

When she fell silent, Kevin held his breath until she met his gaze. "I'm still scared."

"Honestly, so am I, Leah. But not scared enough not to fight for you."

He witnessed the moment that her resistance faded when she smiled. "That's all I needed to hear."

She moved into his lap, framed his face in her palms and kissed him. Kevin couldn't recall feeling so satisfied, so ready to take on the world.

After they parted, she said, "You're going to love Mississippi."

His joy came out in a grin. "Are you tired?"

"Not in the least."

"Are you hungry?"

"Not for food."

"Then I suggest we take my dad's advice and do the rest of our talking in bed."

She pressed a series of kisses along his jaw. "I agree. No matter what went wrong with our relationship before, and what problems we might encounter in the future, we've always gotten lovemaking right and we probably always will."

Kevin couldn't argue with that. "We've done something else right, too."

Together they smiled and at the same time said, "Carly."

LEAH TOOK Kevin by the hand and led him into the room that housed the bed where they'd first made love. A fitting place to begin again, she decided. A merging of the best moments from their past and the promise of more in the future.

Kevin didn't bother to turn down the lights before he began to undress her, and she honestly didn't care. She wanted to see his face, to see every beautiful inch of him when she returned the favor. But instead of dispensing of their clothes, they remained in the center of the room for a long while, simply holding each other until Kevin released her, sat on the edge of the mattress and lowered his head.

Leah moved beside him and leaned her head against his shoulder. "Kevin, what's wrong?"

"I was about to get a condom, then I realized we don't really need one, and that's still killing me inside. Seeing the picture of Logan's son this evening only reinforced how inadequate I feel."

She pressed a kiss against his cheek. "Kevin, being able to biologically create children makes you a sperm donor, not necessarily a good man. Being an incredible father does, and you are an incredible father. Besides, I saw the lab results. There's still hope. After all, I never thought we'd be together again, and look what happened."

"But I want to give you everything, sweetheart. And that's why this is so tough."

Never in her wildest imagination had she believed she would ever see this side of him. Or that she could ever love him more. Yet, in that moment, she did. "You've already given me a beautiful baby, Kevin. And if I've somehow made you doubt yourself, then I'm so sorry." She lay back on the bed and held out her arms to him. "Come here and forget the condom. I don't want anything between us."

He joined her on the bed, and, in very short order, they undressed each other. As always, Kevin used his hands and mouth on her like fine satin, with all the sureness of a man who knew everything about her body. But when she was ready to plead with him to hurry, he moved over her, braced on straight arms and studied her eyes. "Marry me, Leah."

He had her exactly where he wanted her, and he knew it. "You're wicked, Kevin, and you don't always play fair."

"But this time, I'm playing for keeps. I promise I'll always love you, babe."

Leah sensed there was no falseness in that promise. He'd grown in character, but she'd seen glimpses of that from the moment they'd met. And that's why she'd so easily fallen in love with him. Why she loved him so much now. Why she was going to take that final leap of faith. "Yes, I'll marry you, but only if you finish making love to me immediately."

"I'm definitely your man," he said as he eased inside her.

Yes, he was her man. All hers. And he knew her better than any man. He could do things to her that no man ever had.

Their lovemaking was still as passionate, but she noted subtle differences. Kevin held on a little longer, held her a little tighter, both before and after they were totally spent and struggling for air. They stayed tangled together for a long time until he finally rolled to his back and settled her against his chest. For the next few hours, they dozed on and off, but when Leah inadvertently moved even an inch, he brought her back to him. Yet she didn't feel suffocated or stifled in any form or fashion. She felt loved.

Shortly after dawn, Leah opened her eyes to find Kevin watching her. "I thought you'd never wake up," he said.

She stretched and circled her arms around his neck. "Why? Do you have something in mind?"

"I've decided I want to do it before we leave Houston," he said abruptly.

She grinned. "Unlike your brother's fiancée, I don't plan to withhold sexual favors at any point in time."

He frowned. "I meant I want to get *married* before we leave town. I'd like to have the whole family there."

Leah could think of several reasons why that might be a problem. "That's three weeks away, Kevin. How can we plan a wedding when I'm finishing up my fellowship and you're working as well as taking care of our daughter?"

"Trust me. I already have that figured out."

"THANKS for letting us share in your big day, bud."

Kieran shook Kevin's offered hand and grinned. "Not a problem. My wedding is your wedding."

Said wedding had taken place at the estate belonging to Avery Fordyce, Logan's extremely wealthy father-in-law. Kevin had never seen such extensive gardens, not to mention the mansion attached to them. Aside from a rare August rainfall that morning, all had gone as planned with the sunset ceremony. Their dad had served as official best man and the brothers, along with Whit, had filled in as groomsmen. The brides-maids consisted of Mallory and the sisters-in-law and Erica's daughter, Stormy. Assuming the role of flower girls, Mallory's twins had had a great time hurling rose petals at their male cousins who were seated in the audience. And that audience had been made up of in-laws and outlaws in the form of old college buddies and even a couple of old girlfriends who were still family friends. Nothing unusual there. For as long as Kevin could remember, their house had been a haven for kids. Once you got caught up in the O'Brien family web, it was difficult, if not impossible, to break away, even though he'd tried, fortunately without success.

Kevin was amazed that in spite of a short planning time frame, at least for Leah, the ceremony had happened without a hitch, except for an understandably bewildered pastor. "I almost lost it when Reverend Aldine kept getting us mixed up."

"I know," Kieran said. "He came real close to marrying us to the wrong women."

Kevin laughed. "Yeah, and I thought me wearing a tux and you going with the suit and tie would remedy that."

"I told you to get your hair cut, Kev."

He had to admit, they were now the definition of identical twins. At one time he would've rather eaten nails than have anyone mistake him for his brother. Now he was honored. Only one more change in his life to add to all the others. "I'm going to cut it all off before we move. I just thought it might be fun to see who we could confuse, like in the old days."

Kieran loosened his tie and unbuttoned his jacket. "I'm ready for a different kind of fun, and it ain't gonna happen until I get Erica out of here."

Kevin recalled Erica's no-sex-until-the-ceremony rule. That had to suck for his brother. Big-time. "I'm surprised you're walking straight since you've been doing without for weeks."

Kieran smirked. "Actually, that only lasted about four days."

Not at all a shock to Kevin. "You couldn't hold out, could you?"

"Erica couldn't. She came by the house one night and I made her beg for it."

Yeah, right. "For what? About two minutes?"

"Try thirty seconds."

They shared in another laugh before Kieran looked around and said, "Is this a kid menagerie or what?"

Kevin had to agree with that. To their left, Devin's oldest son, Sean, along with Logan's stepson, J.D., were on their hands and knees, playing hide-and-seek beneath the round tables set out for the reception, while Lucy and Maddie wove in and out of the nearby bushes, their skirts hiked up to their knees. Then came the baby section. With Patrick in her arms, Jenna was seated next to Corri, who was playing keep-away-the-cake with her toddler, Emma. And that left Kevin's and Kieran's families. To their right, Stormy had Carly balanced on her hip while Erica and Leah looked on.

Leah…

Kevin would never forget seeing her walk down the aisle wearing the white strapless wedding dress that contrasted with her golden skin. He would always remember the way she looked at him, as though he mattered more than anything else on earth. He'd never seen her look more beautiful, except in the mornings when she'd waken him with a kiss. And also at night when she held their daughter in her arms. He didn't know what he'd done to deserve her, but he refused to question it any longer. He accepted that he'd been blessed and that their time had finally come.

Dermot stood and rapped a spoon on his champagne glass, signaling the moment had arrived for the traditional wedding toast, which earned him a cautioning look from Lucy. Kevin and Kieran rejoined their wives and they all stood together, arms around waists to await the O'Brien patriarch's words of wisdom.

Leah leaned toward Kevin and whispered, "I've heard I should prepare for anything."

"You're right," Kevin said. "With Dad, whatever comes to his mind shoots out of his mouth."

After clearing his throat and garnering everyone's attention, Dermot began. "First, I stand in honor of my youngest lads, once known as the last O'Briens standing, before they took the fall today. To Kieran, may your love for your bride be as big as those blasted biceps. And Erica, may you always be the sun in his morn and the zing in his treadmill. And may you give me another grandchild within the year."

Dermot waited long enough for the laughter to die

down before he held up his glass in Kevin and Leah's direction, his expression much more somber than before. "And to my son, Kevin. I never thought I would live long enough to see you wed. A short year ago, I am certain you did not believe you would live to see it, either. But here you are, with your bonnie bride and your little daughter, having weathered the storms. Although distance may separate us after this day, we know that you must go where your heart leads you, and your heart now belongs to Leah. Kieran, Erica, Kevin and Leah, long life to you all."

As the crowd broke out in "Hear, hear," Kevin smiled at Leah and she smiled back. Then he kissed her to a round of applause. Once they parted, he noticed that Kieran was still engaging in some serious mouth-to-mouth with Erica. "Knock it off, Kieran," he said. "Here comes Mom."

Kieran instantly broke all contact with his wife and looked around, only to find Lucy still seated at the table with their dad. "Real funny, Kev."

Kevin couldn't help but laugh, even when Leah elbowed him in the side and said, "Be nice to your brother. Remember, he's the one who saved us from going to the courthouse."

Erica muffled her own laughter behind her hand before she added, "Leah tells me you've already sold your house, Kevin."

"Yeah, and it's a good thing since we put an offer on a restored farmhouse when we visited her folks last weekend."

Kieran shook his head. "I'm trying to picture you living in a farmhouse in some rural town."

"Noble Oak is only fifteen minutes from Jackson, and it's a huge farmhouse," Leah said. "Three stories with five bedrooms."

Bedrooms that Kevin hoped to fill with kids one day, either biological or adopted. Anything to make Leah happy. "A year ago, I couldn't imagine it either, Kieran."

But like his father, he would willingly go wherever life with Leah and Carly led him. And he was looking forward to it.

EPILOGUE

Mississippi
Three years later

"DADDY, Daddy!"

Kevin spun around in his chair and braced for the curly-headed bundle of exuberance before she landed in his lap. She hugged him hard around the neck then leaned back and stared at him with all the excitement of a major league baseball player who'd just won the series. "Kiss me night."

He popped a kiss on her cheek and set her on her feet about the time a frowning Leah walked in. "Looks like Mom's not happy with you right now, kiddo."

"I've already put her in bed once and told her you'd be in shortly."

Carly went from escape artist to angel in about three seconds. "I kissed Daddy."

Leah pointed behind her. "Now that you've done that, it's time for bed. You have a playdate in the morning."

Carly turned to Kevin again. "Kiss the baby."

"I've already kissed P.J.," he said. "And he's already asleep, which is where you should be."

"Not P.J., silly daddy." She pointed at her mother's stomach. "That baby."

Leah gave him a sly grin as she sauntered over to him. Man, oh, man, she could still send him on a slow burn at any given moment with that look. He lifted the bottom of her blouse with one hand, clasped her hip with the other and pressed his lips against the slight bulge in her belly. This particular baby had been two years in the making following several less-than-pleasant procedures and a little help from science. But success had never tasted so sweet.

He looked up at Leah and presented his own smile. "I'll kiss the baby some more a little later."

Carly giggled and rushed away, seemingly satisfied over the turn of events. Leah climbed into his lap and kissed him in earnest. A down-and-dirty kiss designed to distract him, like she hadn't done that already just by walking into his office. "How long before you come to bed, you sexy stud?"

"If you get out of here, I might make it in fifteen minutes. Twenty minutes, tops. I just have to knock out my final column."

She studied his eyes for a long moment. "Are you sad over leaving the column behind?"

He would be sadder if he'd had to leave her behind. "Maybe a little. But I'm looking forward to the challenge of owning a magazine." He'd purchased and begun to revamp a regional sports magazine. Fortunately, he had a good editorial crew in place, which left him time to care for Carly and their newest addition,

Paul James, the ten-month-old abandoned boy who'd come to them through the free clinic where Leah worked part-time. He'd been born drug-addicted with several other medical problems due to his premature birth. They'd agreed to adopt him even knowing his care involved a long-term commitment. But Kevin didn't shy away from commitment these days.

Leah slid off his lap and blew him a kiss as she backed toward the door. "Hurry up. My hormones are in an uproar."

So was a major part of Kevin's anatomy. "You bet. Now leave before I strip you right here and take you for a ride on the carpet."

"Promises, promises," she said as she closed the door behind her.

Getting back to business, Kevin whirled the chair around and poised his hands on the computer's keyboard. He'd obsessed for days how to end the column he'd written for several years. Then something occurred to him—he was finally ready to finish the column he'd discarded the day that Leah had come back into his life. The same day he'd found out about his daughter.

O'Brien's Sports Scene
August
Final Edition

Four years ago, I learned that facing death can change your life, and not necessarily in a bad way. Knowing you might not survive a disease is like quarterbacking a team during a playoff game, seven points down with fourth and goal to go, twenty seconds away from ending a season. But I was blessed enough to pull through it with the help of family and friends and, most important, the woman who eventually became my wife. You've all seen me write about her before—Leah, the best-looking physician on the face of the earth. Okay, so maybe she wasn't around during my actual battle with the anemia that almost did me in, but she definitely had a hand in saving my life afterward. So did another person who means more to me than I can express.

She's my Hail Mary pass, my three-pointer at the buzzer, my walk-off home run in the tenth inning. More than that, she's the highlight of my day and I can't imagine my life without her.

Her name is Carly, she's three years old and about as tiny as a golf tee. But she's got a big smile and a bigger heart and she can already play catch. Imagine that.

Simply stated, she is the best thing I've ever done. The best part of me. The very best mistake I've ever made.

* * * * *

Harlequin offers a romance for every mood!
See below for a sneak peek
from our paranormal romance line,
Silhouette® Nocturne™.
Enjoy a preview of REUNION by USA TODAY
bestselling author Lindsay McKenna.

Aella closed her eyes and sensed a distinct shift, like movement from the world around her to the unseen world.

She opened her eyes. And had a slight shock at the man standing ten feet away. He wasn't just any man. Her heart leaped and pounded. He reminded her of a fierce warrior from an ancient civilization. Incan? She wasn't sure but she felt his deep power and masculinity.

I'm Aella. Are you the guardian of this sacred site? she asked, hoping her telepathy was strong.

Fox's entire body soared with joy. Fox struggled to put his personal pleasure aside.

Greetings, Aella. I'm the assistant guardian to this sacred area. You may call me Fox. How can I be of service to you, Aella? he asked.

I'm searching for a green sphere. A legend says that the Emperor Pachacuti had seven emerald spheres created for the Emerald Key necklace. He had seven of his priestesses and priests travel the world to hide these spheres from evil forces. It is said that when all seven spheres are found, restrung and worn, that Light will return to the Earth. The fourth sphere is here, at your sacred site. Are you aware of it? Aella held her breath. She loved looking at him, especially his sensual mouth. The desire to kiss him came out of nowhere.

Fox was stunned by the request. *I know of the Emerald Key necklace because I served the emperor at the time it was created. However, I did not realize that one of the spheres is here.*

Aella felt sad. Why? Every time she looked at Fox, her heart felt as if it would tear out of her chest. *May I stay in touch with you as I work with this site?* she asked.

Of course. Fox wanted nothing more than to be here with her. To absorb her ephemeral beauty and hear her speak once more.

Aella's spirit lifted. What *was* this strange connection between them? Her curiosity was strong, but she had more pressing matters. In the next few days, Aella knew her life would change forever. How, she had no idea….

Look for REUNION
by USA TODAY bestselling author
Lindsay McKenna,
available April 2010, only from
Silhouette® Nocturne™.

ROMANCE, RIVALRY
AND A FAMILY REUNITED

THE BRIDES
of
BELLA ROSA

William Valentine and his beloved wife, Lucia, live
a beautiful life together, but when his former love Rosa
and the secret family they had together resurface,
an instant rivalry is formed. Can these families
get through the past and come together as one?

Step into the world of Bella Rosa
beginning this April with

Beauty and the Reclusive Prince
by
RAYE MORGAN

Eight volumes to collect and treasure!

Silhouette Desire

OLIVIA GATES

BILLIONAIRE, M.D.

Dr. Rodrigo Valderrama has it all…
everything but the woman he's secretly
desired and despised. A woman forbidden
to him—his brother's widow.
And she's pregnant.

Cybele was injured in a plane crash
and lost her memory. All she knows is
she's falling for the doctor who has swept her
away to his estate to heal. If only the secrets
in his eyes didn't promise to tear
them forever apart.

Available March wherever you buy books.

Always Powerful, Passionate and Provocative.

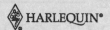

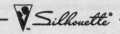

SPECIAL EDITION

**INTRODUCING A BRAND-NEW MINISERIES
FROM *USA TODAY* BESTSELLING AUTHOR**

KASEY MICHAELS

SECOND-CHANCE BRIDAL

At twenty-eight, widowed single mother
Elizabeth Carstairs thinks she's left love behind
forever....until she meets Will Hollingsbrook.
Her sons' new baseball coach is the handsomest
man she's ever seen—and the more time they
spend together, the more undeniable the
connection between them. But can Elizabeth
leave the past behind and open her heart to
a second chance at love?

FIND OUT IN

SUDDENLY A BRIDE

*Available in April
wherever books are sold.*

 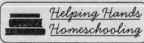

LARGER-PRINT BOOKS!

GET 2 FREE LARGER-PRINT NOVELS PLUS
2 FREE GIFTS!

HARLEQUIN®

Super Romance

Exciting, emotional, unexpected!

HSRLP10

HARLEQUIN
Ambassadors

Want to share your passion for reading Harlequin® Books?

Become a Harlequin Ambassador!

Harlequin Ambassadors are a group of passionate and well-connected readers who are willing to share their joy of reading Harlequin® books with family and friends.

You'll be sent all the tools you need to spark great conversation, including free books!

All we ask is that you share the romance with your friends and family!

You'll also be invited to have a say in new book ideas and exchange opinions with women just like you!

To see if you qualify* to be a Harlequin Ambassador, please visit www.HarlequinAmbassadors.com.

*Please note that not everyone who applies to be a Harlequin Ambassador will qualify. For more information please visit www.HarlequinAmbassadors.com.

Thank you for your participation.

BAP09BPA

HARLEQUIN Super Romance

COMING NEXT MONTH

Available April 13, 2010